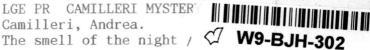

THE
SMELL
OF THE
NIGHT

THE
SMELL
OF THE
NIGHT

Andrea Camilleri
Translated by Stephen Sartarelli

WHEELER
CHIVERS

This Large Print edition is published by Wheeler Publishing, Waterville, Maine USA and by BBC Audiobooks Ltd, Bath, England.

Published in 2006 in the U.S. by arrangement with Viking Penguin, a division of Penguin Group (USA) Inc.

Published in 2006 in the U.K. by arrangement with Pan Macmillan Ltd. Original UK title: SCENT OF THE NIGHT.

U.S. Softcover   1-59722-228-3   (Softcover)
U.K. Hardcover 10: 1 4056 3753 6   (Chivers Large Print)
U.K. Hardcover 13: 978 1 405 63753 4
U.K. Softcover   10: 1 4056 3754 4   (Camden Large Print)
U.K. Softcover   13: 978 1 405 63754 1

Translation copyright © Stephen Sartarelli, 2005

An Inspector Montalbano Mystery.

Originally published in Italian as *L'odore della notte* by Sellerio editore. © 2001 Sellerio editore via Siracusa 50 Palermo.

The text of this Large Print edition is unabridged.
Other aspects of the book may vary from the original edition.

Set in 16 pt. Plantin.

Printed in the United States on permanent paper.

British Library Cataloguing-in-Publication Data available

Library of Congress Cataloging-in-Publication Data

Camilleri, Andrea.
    [Odore della notte. English]
    The smell of the night / by Andrea Camilleri ; translated by Stephen Sartarelli.
        p. (large print) cm.
    ISBN 1-59722-228-3 (lg. print : sc : alk. paper)
    1. Large type books. I. Sartarelli, Stephen, 1954– II. Title.
PQ4863.A38904O3613 2006
853'.914—dc22   2006002207

THE
SMELL
OF THE
NIGHT

1

The shutter outside the wide-open window slammed so hard against the wall that it sounded like a gunshot. Montalbano, who at that moment was dreaming he was in a shoot-out, suddenly woke up, sweaty and at the same time freezing cold. He got up, cursing, and ran to close everything. The north wind was blowing so icy and insistent that instead of brightening the colors of the morning as it had always done, it was carrying them away, erasing them by half, leaving behind only afterimages, or rather faint blotches of the sort made by a Sunday watercolorist. Apparently the summer, which several days earlier had already entered its final throes, had decided during the night to give up the ghost and make way for the season to come, which should have been autumn. Should have been, because, in fact, to judge from the entry it was making, this autumn was already looking like the depths of winter.

Lying back down, Montalbano started elegizing on the disappearance of the transitional seasons. Where had they gone? Swept up like everything else by the ever faster rhythm of human existence, they too had adjusted. Realizing they represented a pause, they had died out, because nowadays no pause can ever be granted by this increasingly frenzied rat race and the endless verbs that feed it: living, eating, studying, fucking, producing, zapping, buying, selling, shitting, dying. Endless verbs that last only, however, a nano-second, the twinkling of an eye. But weren't there once other verbs as well? To think, to meditate, to listen, and — why not? — to loaf, to daydream, to wander . . . Practically with tears in his eyes, Montalbano reminisced about spring and fall clothes and the lightweight duster his father used to wear. Which made him re-alize that, to go to work, he'd have to put on a winter suit.

Making an effort, he got up and opened the armoire where he kept his heavy clothes. The stink of several tons of moth-balls assailed his nostrils. At first it took his breath away, then his eyes started watering and he began to sneeze. He sneezed some twelve times in a row, mucus running down from his nose, head ringing, the pain in his chest growing sharper and sharper. He had forgotten that Adelina, his housekeeper, had forever been waging her own personal, all-out war against moths, from which she always, implacably, emerged defeated.

The inspector gave up. He closed the armoire, went over to the chest of drawers, and pulled out a heavy sweater. Here too Adelina had used chemical weapons, but Montalbano was ready this time and held his breath. He went out on the veranda and laid the sweater down on the table, to air out at least some of the smell. But when, after washing, shaving, and getting dressed, he came back out on the veranda to put it on, the sweater — the very one, brand-new, that Livia had brought him from London — was gone! How was he ever going to explain to her that some son of a bitch had been unable to resist the temptation and had reached out and grabbed it, thank you very much? He imagined exactly how the conversation with his girlfriend would go:

"Well, fancy that! It was to be expected!"

"What do you mean?"

"Because it was a gift from me!"

"What's that got to do with it?"

"It's got everything to do with it! Everything! You never attach any importance to the things I give you! Like the shirt I brought you from —"

"I still have it."

"Of course you still have it! You've never worn it! And what is this, anyway, the famous Inspector Montalbano getting robbed by some two-bit thief? It's enough to make you bury your head in the sand!"

And at that moment he saw it. The sweater, that is. Buffeted away by the north wind, it was rolling along the sand, and as it rolled and rolled, it got closer and closer to the point where the water soaked the beach with each new wave.

Montalbano leapt over the railing and ran, sand filling his socks and shoes, and arrived just in time to snatch the sweater away from an angry wave that looked particularly hungry for that article of clothing.

Walking back to the house, half blinded by the sand whipped into his eyes by the wind, he had no choice but to accept that the sweater had been reduced to a formless, sodden mass of wool. Once inside, the phone rang.

"Hi, darling. How are you? I wanted to let you know that I won't be at home today. I'm going to the beach with a friend."

"You're not going to the office?"

"No, it's a holiday here. Feast of San

Giorgio, patron saint of Genoa."

"The weather's nice up there?"

"Fabulous."

"Well, have fun. Talk to you tonight." This was all he needed to make his day. Here he was, shivering with cold, while Livia would be lying blissfully in the sun. Still further proof that the world was no longer turning the way it used to. Now up north you died of heat, and down south you'd soon be seeing ice, bears, and penguins.

He was getting ready to reopen the armoire, holding his breath, when the phone rang again. He hesitated a moment, but then the thought of the upset stomach he would get from another whiff of moth-balls persuaded him to pick up the receiver.

"Hello?"

"Oh, Chief, Chief!" yelled the tortured, panting voice of Catarella. "Is that you yourself in person, Chief?"

"No."

"Then who is this with whom I'm speaking with?"

"This is Arturo, the inspector's twin brother."

Why was he fucking around with that poor idiot? To vent his bad mood?

"Really?" said Catarella, astonished. "Excuse me, Mr. Twin Brother Arturo, but if the inspector's like roundabout the house, couldja tell 'im I need to talk to him?"

Montalbano let a few seconds go by. Maybe the story he'd just invented could come in handy on another occasion. He wrote down on a piece of paper, *"My brother's name is Arturo,"* then greeted Catarella.

"Here I am! What's up?"

"Oh, Chief, Chief! All hell's breaking out! You know the premises where that broker Gragano gots his office?"

"You mean Gargano?"

"Yes. Why, ain't that what I said? Gragano."

"Never mind. I know where it is. What about it?"

"What's about it's a man with a gun's about it. Sergeant Fazio seen 'im when he was just chancing to be passing by by chance. Looks like he's got a mind to shoot the lady that works there. Says as how he wants all the money back that Gragano stole from 'im or he's gonna kill the lady."

The inspector threw the sweater onto the floor, kicked it under the table, and was out the door. The time it took to get in the car was enough for the north wind to send him into seizures.

★ ★ ★

The *ragioniere* Emanuele Gargano, a tall, handsome, well-dressed forty-year-old with always the right shade of suntan, looked like an American movie star. He belonged to that short-lived breed of businessman that is the fast climber, short-lived because by the age of fifty they're already so worn out that they're ready for the scrap heap (the latter being a favorite expression of theirs). *Ragioniere* Gargano, by his own account, was born in Sicily but had worked a long time in Milan, where, in short, and again by his own account, he'd made a name for himself as a kind of financial miracle worker. Then, judging himself sufficiently famous, he'd decided to go into business for himself in Bologna, where, still by his own account, he'd brought fortune and happiness to dozens of small investors. Some two years back he'd surfaced in Vigàta, to work towards what he called "the economic reawakening of this beloved and unlucky land of ours," and in just a few days he had set up offices in four of the larger towns of Montelusa province. He was a man who was never at a loss for words and had great powers of persuasion over everyone he met, always with a big, reassuring smile on his face. In

13

a week's time — spent racing from one town to the next in a shiny, eye-popping luxury car, a kind of lure for his prey — he had won over about a hundred clients, average age sixty or more, who had turned their life savings over to him. After six months had passed, the aging pensioners were called in to pick up, risking heart attacks on the spot, a twenty-percent return on their investment. The *ragioniere* then summoned all his clients from the surrounding province to Vigàta for a gala dinner, at the end of which he let it be known that, in the coming semester, the returns might even be slightly higher. The news spread and people began lining up at the counters of his various local offices, begging Gargano to take their money. Which the *ragioniere* magnanimously accepted. In this second wave, alongside the oldsters were handfuls of kids anxious to make money as quickly as possible. At the end of the second semester, the returns of the first group of clients increased to twenty-three percent. It was smooth sailing for a while, with a stiff tail wind, but then, one day towards the end of the fourth semester, Emanuele Gargano failed to show up. His agencies' employees and clients waited two days and then decided to phone Bologna, where the general management office of "King Midas Associates" — the name of the *ragioniere*'s investment firm — was supposedly located. Nobody answered. A quick investigation led to the discovery that the premises of King Midas Associates, leased by said firm, had been turned back over to their legal owner, who for his part was furious that the rent hadn't been paid for many months. After a week of pointless searches yielded not a trace of Gargano in or around Vigàta, and after several riotous assaults on the agencies by people who had invested their money with Midas, two schools of thought emerged concerning the *ragioniere*'s mysterious disappearance.

The first had it that Emanuele Gargano, after changing his name, must have moved to an island in Oceania, where he was now living it up with beautiful half-naked women, laughing all the while at those who'd placed their trust and savings in his hands.

The second found it more likely that the *ragioniere* had carelessly made off with some mafioso's money and was now serving as fertilizer six feet underground or as fish feed in the local waters.

In all of Montelusa province there was

one woman, however, who saw things differently. Only one, and her name was Mariastella Cosentino.

Fiftyish, stocky, and homely, Mariastella had applied for a job at Midas's Vigàta agency and, after a brief but intense meeting with the boss in person, had been taken on. That's how the story went. Yet however brief the meeting, it had been long enough for the woman to fall hopelessly in love with the *ragioniere*. And while this was the second job for Mariastella — who, after getting a degree in accounting, had stayed home for many years to help out her parents and later her widowed father, who'd become more and more demanding before he died — it was, in fact, her first love. For Mariastella had been promised since birth to a distant cousin she'd never seen except in photographs and never known in person because he died of an unknown illness in his youth. Things were different this time, however, and Mariastella had not only seen her beloved alive and speaking on several occasions, but had even, one morning, got so close as to smell the scent of his aftershave. That incident drove her to do something audacious — so audacious, indeed, that she would never in the world have thought herself capable of it. She took the bus to Fiacca to visit a relative who owned a perfume shop and, after smelling bottle after bottle, found the aftershave used by her beloved. She bought a flask of it, which she kept in the drawer of her bedside table. On certain nights, when she woke up alone in bed, alone in the large, empty house and overcome with distress, she would uncork it and inhale the scent, and this allowed her to go back to sleep, murmuring, "Good night, my love."

Mariastella was convinced that Emanuele Gargano had not run away with all the money entrusted to him, much less been killed in some row with the Mafia. When questioned by Mimì Augello (Montalbano had no desire to get involved in the case, claiming he didn't understand a damn thing about money matters), Miss Cosentino had stated that, in her opinion, the *ragioniere* must be suffering from temporary amnesia and would reappear sooner or later and set all the wagging tongues to rest. And she'd said this with such lucid fervor that Augello was in danger of believing it himself.

Armed with her faith in Gargano's honesty, Mariastella would open up the office every morning, sit down and wait for her love to return. Everyone in town laughed at her. Everyone, that is, who hadn't had any dealings with the *ragioniere,* since those who'd lost their money were not in a laughing mood. The day before, Gallo had told Montalbano that Miss Cosentino had even gone to the bank to pay, out of her own pocket, the rent that was due on the office. So why had the guy now threatening her with a gun got it in his head to take it out on her? Poor thing, she had nothing to do with the whole affair. And why, in fact, had the distraught investor come up with his brilliant idea so late, some thirty days after Gargano's disappearance, in other words at a time when most of the *ragioniere*'s victims had resigned themselves to the worst? Montalbano belonged to the first school of thought, the one that believed that the *ragioniere* had split after screwing everybody, and he felt very sorry for Mariastella Cosentino. Every time he happened to pass in front of the agency and saw her sitting there calmly behind the counter, he felt an ache in his heart that would stay with him for the rest of the day.

There were about thirty people in front of the King Midas office, heatedly talking and wildly gesticulating, and kept at bay by three municipal policemen. Recognizing the inspector, they surrounded him.

"Is it true there's a man with a gun inside?"

"Who is he? Who is he?"

He forced his way through the crowd, shoving and yelling, and finally reached the entrance to the building. But here he stopped, slightly bewildered. Inside he saw, recognizing them from behind, Mimì Augello, Fazio, and Galluzzo, who looked as if they were involved in some strange kind of ballet: first bending their upper bodies to the right, then to the left, then taking one step forward, one step back. He opened the glass outer door without a sound and got a better look at the scene. The office consisted of a single, spacious room divided in two by a wooden counter with a sheet of glass and a teller's window on top. Beyond this partition were four empty desks. Mariastella Cosentino was sitting at her usual place behind the teller's window, very pale, but calm and composed. One came and went between the two sections of the office through a small wooden door in the partition itself.

The assailant, or whatever he was — Montalbano didn't know how to define him — was standing right in the little doorway between the two sections, so that he could keep his gun trained simultaneously on Mariastella and the three policemen. He was an old man of about eighty whom the inspector recognized at once, a respected land surveyor named Salvatore Garzullo. Partly because of nervous tension, partly because of fairly advanced Parkinson's, the pistol — which dated surely back to the days of Buffalo Bill and the Sioux — was shaking so badly in the old man's hands that whenever he aimed it at one of the inspector's men, they all took fright because they couldn't tell where an eventual shot might end up.

"I want back the money that son of a bitch stole from me, or I'm going to kill the lady!"

The land surveyor had been yelling this same demand without variation for over an hour, and by now he was getting worn out and hoarse. More than speaking, he seemed to be making gargling sounds.

Montalbano took three resolute steps, walked past the line formed by his men, and held out his hand to the old man, a smile beaming across his face.

"Dear Mr. Garzullo, what a pleasure to see you! How are you?"

"I'm doing all right, thanks," said Garzullo, confused.

But he recovered himself immediately

when he saw Montalbano about to take another step towards him.

"Stay where you are or I'll shoot!"

"For heaven's sake, Inspector, be careful!" Miss Cosentino said in a steady voice. "If someone has to be sacrificed for Mr. Gargano, let it be me. I'm ready!"

Instead of bursting out laughing at the melodrama of these lines, Montalbano felt enraged. If he could have had Gargano in his hands at that moment, he would have slapped his face to a bloody pulp.

"Let's not be foolish! Nobody here is going to be sacrificed!"

Then, turning back to the land surveyor, he began his improvisation.

"Excuse me, Mr. Garzullo, but where were you yesterday evening?"

"What the hell is it to you?" the old man retorted combatively.

"For your own good, answer me."

The old man pursed his lips, then finally decided to open his mouth.

"I'd just got back home. I was four months in Palermo hospital, and that was where they told me Gargano ran off with my money. Everything I had, after a life of hard work!"

"So yesterday evening you did not turn on the television?"

"I didn't wanna hear any of that bullshit."

"So *that's* why you don't know!" said Montalbano, triumphant.

"What is it I'm supposed to know?" asked Garzullo, dumbfounded.

"*Ragioniere* Gargano's been arrested."

The inspector looked out of the corner of his eye at Mariastella. He was expecting a scream, or any reaction at all; but the woman remained immobile, looking more confused than convinced.

"Really?" said the old man.

"Word of honor," said Montalbano, in a superb performance. "They arrested him and confiscated twelve big suitcases stuffed full of money. They're going to start giving the money back to its rightful owners this very morning in Montelusa, at the Prefecture. Do you have the receipt for the amount you gave to Gargano?"

"I sure do!" said the old man, tapping with his free hand against his jacket pocket, where he kept his wallet.

"So there's no problem, it's all been settled," said Montalbano.

He walked up to the old man, took the pistol out of his hand, and set it down on the counter.

"Think I could go to the Prefecture tomorrow?" Garzullo asked. "I'm not feeling so well."

He would have collapsed onto the floor if the inspector hadn't been ready to catch him.

"Fazio and Galluzzo, quick, put him in the car and take him to the hospital."

The two policemen picked up the old man, who, as he was being carried past Montalbano, managed to say: "Thanks for everything."

"Not at all, you're very welcome," said Montalbano, feeling like the biggest heel in the world.

2

Mimì meanwhile had rushed over to help Miss Mariastella, who, though she remained seated, had started swaying in place like a tree in a windstorm.

"Want me to get you anything from the café?"

"A glass of water, thank you."

At that moment they heard a burst of applause from outside, accompanied by shouts of "Bravo! Long live old man Garzullo!" Apparently many of the people in the crowd had been swindled by Gargano.

"But why do they hate him so much?" the woman asked as Mimì was leaving.

She was wringing her hands and had now turned, in reaction, from pale to tomato-red.

"Well, they've probably got their reasons," the inspector replied diplomatically. "You know better than I that the *ragioniere* has disappeared."

"Of course, but why must people immediately think the worst? He might have lost his memory in a car accident, or after a fall, I don't know . . . I even took the liberty of telephoning . . ."

She broke off, shaking her head disconsolately.

"Never mind," she said, concluding her thought.

"Tell me who it was you called."

"Do you watch television?"

"Sometimes. Why?"

"I'd heard there was a program called *Anybody Seen 'Em?*, which is about missing persons. So I got their telephone number and —"

"I get the picture. What did they tell you?"

"They said they couldn't do anything, since I was unable to give them the necessary information, age, place of disappearance, photographs, that sort of thing."

Silence fell. Mariastella's hands had become a single, inextricable knot. Montalbano's accursed police instincts, which had been dozing off, suddenly popped awake for no apparent reason.

"You, signorina, must also take into account the fact that a lot of money disappeared with Mr. Gargano. We're talking about billions and billions of lire, you know."

"Yes, I know."

"And you haven't the slightest idea where —"

"I only know that he invested that money. Where and in what he invested it, I can't say."

"And you and he. . . . ?"

Mariastella's face became a blaze of fire.

"What. . . . what do you mean?"

"Has he contacted you in any way since his disappearance?"

"If he had, I would have mentioned it to Inspector Augello, when he questioned me. But I'll repeat to you what I said to your assistant: Emanuele Gargano has only one goal in life, and that is to make others happy."

"I have no problem believing that," said Montalbano.

And he meant it. He was convinced that *ragioniere* Gargano was making some high-class prostitutes, nightclub owners, casino managers, and luxury-car dealers very happy on some lost Polynesian island.

Mimì Augello returned with a bottle of mineral water, a few paper cups, and his cell phone glued to his ear.

"Yessir, yessir, I'll put him on right away."

He handed the contraption to the inspector.

"It's for you. The commissioner."

What a pain in the ass! Relations between Montalbano and Commissioner Bonetti-Alderighi could hardly be said to be characterized by mutual esteem and sympathy. If he was calling the inspector, it meant there was some unpleasant matter to discuss. And Montalbano, at that moment, had no desire for any such thing.

"At your service, Mr. Commissioner."

"Come here immediately."

"Give me an hour at the most, and I'll —"

"Montalbano, you may be Sicilian, but surely you studied Italian at school? Don't you know the meaning of the adverb 'immediately'?"

"Just a second, I'll need to think that over. Ah, yes. It means, 'Without interval of time.' Am I right, Mr. Commissioner?"

"Spare me the wit. You have exactly fifteen minutes to get here to Montelusa."

He hung up.

"Mimì, I have to go see the commissioner right away. Grab Garzullo's pistol and take it in to headquarters. And Miss Cosentino, allow me a word of advice: Close this office right now and go home."

"Why?"

"Because in a very short while, you see, everyone in town will know about Mr.

Garzullo's stroke of genius. And it's not beyond the realm of possibility that some idiot will repeat the stunt, and that this time it will be somebody younger and more dangerous."

"No," said a resolute Mariastella. "I'm not leaving this place. What if Mr. Gargano were to return? He'd find nobody here."

"Imagine the disappointment!" said Montalbano, furious. "And another thing: Do you intend to press charges against Mr. Garzullo?"

"Absolutely not."

"So much the better."

The road to Montelusa was jammed with traffic, and Montalbano's dark mood worsened as a result. He was, moreover, in a wretched state from all the sand scratching between his socks and skin, collar and neck. At one point, about a hundred yards up the road, on the left and therefore on the opposite side, he saw the "Trucker's Rest Stop," where he knew they made first-rate coffee. When he was nearly parallel to the spot, he put on his blinker and turned. A riot, a pandemonium of screeching brakes, blaring horns, shouts, insults, and curses ensued. By some miracle he reached the parking lot in front of the restaurant unscathed, got out of the car, and went inside. The first thing he saw were two people he immediately recognized, even though they had their backs to him. It was Fazio and Galluzzo, each knocking back a glass of cognac, or so, at least, it looked to him. Cognac, at that hour of the morning? He wedged himself in between the two and ordered a coffee from the barman. Recognizing his voice, Fazio and Galluzzo turned around with a start.

"To your health," said Montalbano.

"No . . . it's just that . . . ," Galluzzo began, trying to justify himself.

"We were feeling a little upset," said Fazio.

"And we needed something strong," Galluzzo added.

"Upset? Why?"

"Poor Mr. Garzullo died! He had a heart attack," said Fazio. "By the time we got to the hospital he was unconscious. We called the attendants and they rushed him inside. After we parked the car we went straight back in, and they told us. . . ."

"It shook us up," said Galluzzo.

"I feel a little shook up myself . . . ," Montalbano admitted. "Listen, I want you to do something. Find out if he had any relatives and, if not, track down some close friend and report to me after I get back from Montelusa."

Fazio and Galluzzo said good-bye and left. Montalbano drank his coffee calmly, then he remembered that the Trucker's Rest Stop was also known for selling a *tumazzo* goat cheese which was supposed to be delicious, although nobody knew who made it. He immediately wanted some and went over to that part of the counter where, along with the *tumazzo,* there was a variety of sausages and salami on display. The inspector was tempted to drop a lot of money, but managed to control himself and bought only a small round of goat cheese.

When it came time to pull out from the parking lot and onto the road, he realized this would be no easy feat. The line of trucks and cars was packed tight, with no openings in sight. After waiting five minutes, he saw daylight and joined the procession. All the while he was driving, a thought kept trying to form in his mind, but he was unable to give it any shape, and this bothered him. And thus, without even noticing, he found himself back in Vigàta.

What now? Take the road back to

Montelusa and show up at the commissioner's late? With nothing more to lose, he decided he might as well go home to Marinella, take a shower, change into some better clothes, and, all clean and fresh, face the commissioner with a clear head. As the water streamed over him, the thought came into focus.

Half an hour later, he pulled up in front of headquarters, got out of his car, and went inside. The moment he entered, he was deafened by Catarella's shouting; actually, more than shouting, it was something between barking and whinnying.

"Aaaahhhh, Chief, Chief, Chief! You're here? Here?"

"Yes, Cat, I'm here. What's wrong?"

"What's wrong is that his honor the c'mishner is making like a pack of demons, Chief! He called here five times! Each time madder than the last!"

"Tell him to relax."

"I couldn't talk to his honor the c'mishner like that! Never in a million years! That'd be a terrible act of disrespeck! Whaddo I tell 'im if he calls again?"

"Tell him I'm not here."

"Nossirree, I won't! I can't be telling lies to his honor the c'mishner!"

"Then let him talk to Inspector Augello."

He opened the door to Mimì's office.

"What'd the commissioner want?" asked Mimì.

"I don't know, I haven't been to see him yet."

"Jesus Christ! And who's gonna deal with him now?"

"You are. You're going to call him and tell him that as I was rushing to see him, I was driving too fast and went off the road. Nothing serious, just three stitches on my forehead. Tell him I'm feeling better now, and that I'll fulfill my obligation this afternoon. Fill his ears with chatter. Then come and see me."

He went into his office and was immediately followed by Fazio.

"I wanted to tell you we found Garzullo's granddaughter."

"Well done. How'd you do it?"

"We didn't have to do anything, Chief. She came forward on her own. She was worried because he wasn't home when she went to see him this morning. She waited a bit, then decided to come here. I had to give her the triple bad news."

"Triple?"

"Come on, Inspector. First: she didn't

know her grandfather had lost all his savings to Gargano; second: she didn't know her grandfather had started acting out scenes from gangster movies; and third: she didn't know her grandfather was dead."

"How did the poor thing take it?"

"Badly. Especially when she found out he'd let somebody piss away all the money he'd saved, which was supposed to go to her when he died."

Fazio went out and Augello came in, wiping his neck with a handkerchief.

"He sure made me sweat, that commissioner! In the end he told me to tell you that unless you're on the very brink of death, he'll be expecting you this afternoon."

"Sit down, Mimì, and give me the low-down on *ragioniere* Gargano."

"Now?"

"Now. What's the matter, you in a hurry?"

"No, it's just that the story's sort of complicated."

"Make it nice and simple for me."

"All right. But I can really only tell you the half of it, because we've only been dealing with the part that falls under our authority. Those were the commissioner's orders. The meat of the case has been handled by Inspector Guarnotta, the fraud specialist."

Looking each other in the eye, they couldn't help but burst out laughing. It was well known that, two years earlier, Amelio Guarnotta had let himself be persuaded into buying many shares in a company that was going to turn the Colosseum, after its privatization, into a luxury apartment complex.

"Anyway, Emanuele Gargano was born in February of 1960 in Fiacca and got his accounting degree in Milan."

"Why Milan? Had his family moved there?"

"No, his family moved to heaven in a car crash. And since he was an only child, he was adopted, in a manner of speaking, by his father's brother, a bachelor and bank manager. Once Gargano received his degree, his uncle got him a job at the same bank. About ten years later, after his protector passed away and left him alone in the world, he went to work for an investment firm and showed a great deal of promise. Three years ago he quit the firm and opened King Midas Associates in Bologna, with himself as the sole proprietor. And this is where things start to get weird.

34

Or at least that's what I'm told, since this part doesn't come under our authority."

"What's weird about it?"

"First of all, the entire staff of King Midas of Bologna consists of a single employee, a woman rather like our own Miss Cosentino; and secondly, the firm's entire turnover amounts to about two billion lire over three years. Peanuts."

"A cover."

"Of course. But a preventive cover, with a view in mind to the big scam Gargano was planning to pull off down here."

"Could you explain this scam to me?"

"It's simple. Let's say you give me a million lire to invest for you, and I, six months later, give you back a profit of two hundred thousand lire. Twenty percent. That's a really high rate of return, and the word gets around. Along comes another friend of yours who invests another million with me. At the end of the next six months, I give you another two hundred thousand lire return, and the same to your friend. At this point I decide to skip town, making off with a gain of one million four hundred thousand lire. Subtract, say, another four hundred thousand in expenses, and in the end I've still pocketed a cool million. To make a long story short, Gargano, according to Guarnotta, raked in over twenty billion lire this way."

"Damn. It's all the television's fault," commented Montalbano.

"What's television got to do with it?"

"Everything. There's not a single TV news program that doesn't bombard you with noise about the stock market, the Mibtel, the Dow Jones, the Nasdaq, the Nisdick. . . . People don't know the first thing about it, but they're impressed. They know it's risky, but they also know you can make a lot of money, and so they rush into the arms of the first swindler they run across. Lemme play too, I wanna play. . . . Skip it. What's your impression?"

"I think — and Guarnotta does too — that Gargano's biggest clients must have included some mafioso who knocked him off when he realized he'd been had."

"So you don't subscribe to the school of thought that has Gargano living happily ever after on some South Sea island?"

"No. What do you think?"

"I think you and Guarnotta are a couple of dumbfucks."

"Why?"

"I'll tell you why. But first you have to find me a mafioso stupid enough not to realize that Gargano's scam is pretty crude.

36

If anything, the mafioso would have forced Gargano to make him a senior partner in the business. And anyway, how would this hypothetical mafioso have intuited that Gargano was about to rip him off?"

"I don't understand."

"We're a little slow today, eh, Mimì? Think. How did the mafioso guess that Gargano wasn't going to show up to pay the dividends? When was he last seen?"

"I don't know, about a month ago, in Bologna. He told his secretary he was leaving for Sicily the next day."

"How's that?"

"He said he was leaving for Sicily the next day," Augello repeated.

Montalbano slammed his hand against the table.

"Has Catarella become contagious or something? Are you becoming a cretin too? I was asking you by what means of transport he would be coming to Sicily. Plane? Train? On foot?"

"The woman didn't know. But every time he came to Vigàta, he would drive around in a fully equipped Alfa 166, the kind with a computer on the dashboard."

"Was this car ever found?"

"No."

"He had a computer in his car, but I

didn't see a single one in his office. Strange."

"He had two. Guarnotta had them confiscated."

"And what did he find out?"

"They're still working on them."

"How many employees did Gargano have working for him at the local branch, apart from Miss Cosentino?"

"A couple of kids, the kind who nowadays know everything about the Internet and all that stuff. One of them, Giacomo Pellegrino, has a degree in business economics; the other's a girl, Michela Manganaro, and she's also working on a degree at business economics. They live in Vigàta."

"I want to talk to them. Get me their phone numbers. Have them on my desk by the time I get back from Montelusa."

Augello darkened, stood up, and left the room without a word.

Montalbano understood. Mimì was afraid he would take the case away from him. Or, worse yet, he was worried the inspector had come up with some brilliant idea that would steer the investigation in the right direction. But that wasn't at all the case. How could Montalbano tell him that he was acting on an insubstantial impression, a pale shadow, a tenuous thread ready to break at the slightest breath of wind?

At the Trattoria San Calogero the inspector wolfed down two servings of grilled fish, one right after the other, as his first and second courses. Afterward he took a long, digestive stroll along the jetty, all the way out to the lighthouse. There he hesitated a moment, undecided as to whether he should sit down on his customary rock. The wind was too strong and too cold and, anyway, he thought it was probably better to get the commissioner out of the way.

Arriving in Montelusa, instead of going immediately to the commissioner's office, he paid a visit to the editorial offices of the Free Channel. They told him his friend, the newsman Nicolò Zito, was out on assignment. But Annalisa, the all-purpose secretary, made herself available.

"Have you done any reports on Emanuele Gargano, the investment banker, at the Free Channel?"

"On his disappearance, you mean?"

"Even before that."

"We have as many as you want."

"Could you tape for me the ones you

consider the most important? And could I have them by tomorrow afternoon?"

Leaving his car in the parking lot of Montelusa Central Police, he entered through a side door and waited for the elevator. There were three people waiting with him. One of them, an assistant commissioner, was an acquaintance, and they greeted each other. Montalbano got in ahead of the others. When all of them, including a man who'd rushed in at the last second, were inside, the assistant commissioner raised his index finger to press the button but never got any further, paralyzed by a screaming Montalbano.

"Stop!"

They all turned round to look at him, half dumbstruck, half terrified.

"Excuse me! Excuse me!" the inspector continued, clearing the way with his elbows.

Exiting the elevator, he ran to his car, turned on the ignition, and drove off, cursing the saints. He'd completely forgotten that Mimì was supposed to tell the commissioner he'd got a couple of stitches in his forehead. His only choice was to return to Vigàta and have a pharmacist friend put a bandage on him.

3

He returned to Montelusa Central with a broad gauze bandage wrapped around his head, making him look like a Vietnam War survivor. In the waiting room outside the commissioner's office, he ran into the latter's cabinet chief, Dr. Lattes, whom everybody called "Caffè-Lattes" for his cloying manner. Lattes noticed — he could hardly have done otherwise — the enormous bandage.

"What happened to you?"

"A minor auto accident. Nothing serious."

"Thank the Lord!"

"I already have, thanks."

"And how's the family, dear Inspector? Everyone all right?"

Everybody and his dog knew that Montalbano was an orphan, unmarried, and with no secret children out of wedlock, either. And yet, without fail, Lattes always asked him the same exact question. And the inspector, with similar obstinacy, never disappointed him.

"They're all fine, thank the Lord. How are yours?"

"Fine, fine, thank the heavens," said Lattes, pleased that Montalbano had afforded him the chance to add a little variation to the theme. "So," he continued, "what pleasant task brings you this way?"

What? Hadn't the commissioner told the chief of his cabinet that he'd been summoned to see him? Was it such a secret matter?

"Commissioner Bonetti-Alderighi phoned me, said he wanted to see me."

"Oh, really?" Lattes marveled. "I'll tell the commissioner at once that you're here."

He knocked discreetly on the commissioner's door, went inside, closed the door behind him. A moment later the door opened and Lattes reappeared, his face transformed and no longer smiling.

"You can go in now," he said.

Walking past him, Montalbano tried to look him in the eye but was unable to. The cabinet chief was keeping his head down. Shit. It must really be serious. But what had he done wrong? He went in. Lattes closed the door behind him, and to Montalbano it seemed as if the lid of a coffin had just been lowered over him.

The commissioner, who whenever he received Montalbano mounted a stage-set for the occasion, had resorted this time to lighting effects similar to those one might see in a black-and-white film by Fritz Lang. The shutters were tightly closed, the shades all pulled down except one, letting a thin ray of sun filter through, the purpose of which was to slice the room in two. The only source of illumination was a low, mushroom-shaped table lamp, which shed its light on the papers spread out over the commissioner's desk but kept his face entirely in darkness. Based on the decor, Montalbano became convinced that he was about to be subjected to an interrogation somewhere between the kind once carried out by the Holy Inquisition and the kind in fashion with the SS.

"Come in."

The inspector stepped forward. In front of the desk were two chairs, but he did not sit down, and in any case the commissioner had not invited him to do so. Montalbano did not greet his superior, and neither did Bonetti-Alderighi, for his part, greet him. The commissioner kept reading the papers he had before him.

A good five minutes passed. The inspector then decided to counterattack. If he did not take the initiative, Bonetti-Alderighi was liable to leave him standing there in the dark, literally and figuratively, for several hours. He slipped a hand into his jacket pocket, extracted a pack of cigarettes, took one out, put it between his lips, and fired up his lighter. The commissioner leapt out of his chair, the little flame having had the same effect as the blast of a *lupara*.

"What are you doing?!" he cried, looking up in terror from his papers.

"I'm lighting a cigarette."

"Put that thing out at once! Smoking is strictly forbidden here!"

Without a word, the inspector extinguished the lighter. But he continued to hold it in his hand, just as he continued to hold the cigarette between his lips. He had, however, achieved the result he'd wanted, for the commissioner, frightened by the threat of the lighter about to spring into action, went straight to the heart of the matter.

"Montalbano, I've unfortunately been forced to stick my nose into some dossiers on a rather malodorous investigation of yours from a few years ago, before I became commissioner of Montelusa Police."

"Your nose is too sensitive for the line of work you're in."

The comment had slipped out; he hadn't managed to hold it in. And he immediately regretted it. He saw Bonetti-Alderighi's hand come into the cone of light cast by the lamp and clutch the edge of the desk, knuckles pale from the effort he was making to control himself. Montalbano feared the worst, but the commissioner restrained himself. He resumed speaking in a tense voice.

"I'm talking about the case of that Tunisian prostitute who was later found dead, and who had a son by the name of François."

The boy's name cut straight to his heart like a dagger. My God, François! How long had it been since he'd seen him? He resolved, however, to pay close attention to the commissioner's words; he didn't want the surge of emotion to overwhelm him and leave him unable to defend himself. For it was clear that Bonetti-Alderighi was about to begin making accusations. He tried to recall to mind all the details of that distant case. Want to bet that Lohengrin Pera, that son of a bitch from the Secret Service, had found a way to take his revenge after all these years? But the commissioner's next words threw him for a loop.

"Apparently you had originally intended

45

to get married and adopt this child. Is this true?"

"Yes, it's true," replied the inspector, stunned.

What the hell did this personal detail have to do with the investigation? And how did Bonetti-Alderighi know these things?

"Good. Later you apparently changed your mind about the adoption. And thereafter François was entrusted to the care of a sister of your second-in-command, Inspector Domenico Augello. Is that correct?"

What was this goddamn son of a bitch getting at?

"Yes, that's correct."

Montalbano was feeling more and more worried. He knew neither why the commissioner was so interested in this story, nor from what angle the inevitable blow was going to come.

"All in the family, eh?"

Bonetti-Alderighi's sardonic tone contained a clear yet inexplicable insinuation. What on earth was going through the imbecile's head?

"Listen, Mr. Commissioner. It seems to me you've formed a clear idea of an affair I scarcely remember anymore. Whatever the case, please weigh your words carefully."

"Don't you dare threaten me!" Bonetti-

Alderighi screamed hysterically, bringing his fist down hard on the desk, which reacted with a *crack*. "Come on, tell me: what ever happened to the booklet?"

"What booklet?"

He honestly had no recollection of any booklet.

"Don't play dumb with me, Montalbano!"

It was those very words, *Don't play dumb,* that finally set him off. He hated clichés and stock phrases; they aroused an uncontrollable rage in him.

This time it was his turn to bring his fist down on the desk, which reacted with a *crick-crack*.

"What goddamn booklet are you babbling about?"

"Hey, hey!" the commissioner sneered. "Nose not too clean, Montalbano?"

He felt that if, after the *playing dumb* and the *nose not too clean,* the commissioner were to come out with another of these expressions, he was going to grab Bonetti-Alderighi by the neck and strangle him to death. By some miracle he managed not to react or even to open his mouth.

"But before we get to the booklet," the commissioner resumed, "let's talk about the boy, the prostitute's son. You, without telling anyone, brought this orphan into your house. That's illegal confinement of a minor, Montalbano! There's a court for these kinds of things, don't you know that? There are special judges for minors, don't you know that? You're supposed to follow the law, not avoid it! This is not the Wild West!"

Exhausted, he paused. Montalbano didn't breathe a word.

"And that's not all! Not content with this fine exploit, you make a present of the boy to your assistant's sister, as if he were some kind of object! This is the stuff of heartless people, the stuff of actionable offenses! But we'll come back to that part. It gets worse. The prostitute possessed a bank booklet, a passbook showing half a billion lire on deposit. At some point, this booklet passed into your hands. And then it disappeared! What happened to it? Did you split the money with your friend and accomplice Domenico Augello?"

Very slowly, Montalbano placed his hand on the desk; then, also very slowly, he leaned his upper body forward; and, very slowly, he brought his head into the cone of light made by the lamp. Bonetti-Alderighi got scared. Half lit, Montalbano's face looked exactly like an African mask, the sort that might be worn before a human sacrifice. After all — the commissioner probably thought, feeling a chill — it's not that far from Sicily to Africa. The inspector looked him deep in the eye, then began to speak very slowly and very softly.

"I'm gonna tell you man to man. Forget about the kid. Leave him out of this. Got that? He's been properly adopted by Augello's sister and her husband. Leave him out of this. For your personal vendettas, your personal bullshit, there's always me, and that should be enough. Agreed?"

The commissioner didn't answer. Fear and rage made it hard for him to speak.

"Agreed?" Montalbano asked again.

And the lower, the calmer, the slower his voice became, the more Bonetti-Alderighi sensed the barely restrained violence behind it.

"Agreed," he finally said in a faint voice.

Montalbano withdrew his face from the light and stood up straight.

"May I ask, Mr. Commissioner, where you got all this information?"

Montalbano's sudden change in tone, now formal and slightly obsequious, so shocked the commissioner that he ended up saying what he had resolved not to say.

"Somebody wrote to me."

Montalbano understood immediately.

"An anonymous letter, right?"

"Well, let's say unsigned."

"You should be ashamed of yourself," said the inspector, turning and heading for the door, deaf to the commissioner's shouting.

"Montalbano, come back here!"

He wasn't some kind of dog that obeyed all commands. He tore the useless wrapping off his head, enraged. In the corridor he ran straight into Lattes, who stammered:

"I . . . think . . . the commissioner's calling you."

"I think he is too."

At that moment Lattes realized that Montalbano was no longer wearing the bandage and that his head was intact.

"You're already healed?"

"Didn't you know the commissioner's a miracle worker?"

The amazing thing about this whole business, he thought, hands squeezing the steering wheel as he drove back towards Marinella, was that he wasn't upset at the person who'd written the anonymous letter, surely a secret vendetta on the part of Lohengrin Pera, the only one in a position to reconstruct the story of François and his mother. And he wasn't even upset at the commissioner. The rage he was feeling was against himself. How could he have forgotten so utterly about the passbook for the five hundred million lire? He'd entrusted it to a friend of his, a notary — this much he remembered perfectly — so that he could manage the money and turn it over to François as soon as he came of age. He also remembered, though rather vaguely this time, that about ten days later the same notary had sent him a receipt. But he had no idea where he'd stuck it. The worst of it was that he'd never made any mention of this passbook to either Mimì Augello or his sister. Which meant that Mimì, though totally unaware of anything, might well be called to task by Bonetti-Alderighi's fertile imagination, when in fact he was innocent as Christ.

In scarcely an hour's time he made his house look like a place that had been visited by skillful, conscientious burglars. Drawers pulled completely out of his desk, the papers inside strewn across the floor, next to books half opened, skimmed and abused. In the bedroom both night tables were thrown wide open, ditto the armoire and dresser, their contents scattered over the bed and the chairs. Montalbano looked and kept on looking, and finally became convinced that never in a million years would he succeed in finding what he was searching for. Then, just when he'd given up hope, inside a box in the dresser's bottom drawer, next to a photo of his mother, who'd died before an image of the living person could form in his memory, together with a photo of his father and a few of his rare letters, Montalbano found the envelope sent him by the notary, opened it, took out the document, read it, reread it, went out of the house, got in his car, remembered that in one of the first buildings at the edge of Vigàta there was a tobacco shop with a photocopier, copied the document, got back in his car, went home, took fright at the shambles he'd made of his house, started looking for a sheet of paper and an envelope, cursing all the while, found these, sat down at his desk, and wrote:

Esteemed Commissioner
of Vigàta Police,
  Given that you are inclined to lending an ear to anonymous letters, I won't sign this one. Enclosed herewith is a copy of a receipt from the notary

Giulio Carlentini, clarifying the position of Inspector Salvo Montalbano. The original is of course in the possession of the present writer and may be viewed upon polite request.

Signed,
a friend

He got back in his car, went to the post office, sent the letter registered mail with return receipt requested, left, leaned over to open his car door, and froze in that position like somebody suddenly seized by one of those violent back spasms that, at the slightest move, stab you like a knife, and all you can do is stand perfectly still in the hope that some miracle might, at least momentarily, make the pain go away. What had made the inspector blanch was the sight of a woman passing by at that moment, apparently on her way to a nearby delicatessen. It was none other than Mariastella Cosentino, vestal of the temple of *ragioniere* Gargano. Having closed up the agency at the end of the afternoon shift, she was buying groceries before going home. The sight of Mariastella Cosentino had brought to mind a chilling thought, followed by an even more chilling question: What if, by some terrible luck, the notary had invested François's money with Gargano's firm? If so, the cash by now had already evaporated and headed towards the South Seas, which meant not only that the kid would never see a lira of his mother's estate, but also that he, Montalbano, after having just sent that taunting letter to the commissioner, would have an awfully hard time explaining the money's disappearance. Try as he might to say he had nothing to do with it, the commissioner would never believe him. At the very least he would think the inspector had plotted with the notary to split the poor orphan's five hundred million lire.

He managed to rouse himself, opened the car door, and sped off, screeching the tires the way policemen and imbeciles often do, in the direction of the notary Carlentini's office. There, he raced up two flights of stairs, getting winded in the process. The door was closed, and outside was a small sign posting the office hours. It was an hour after closing time, but somebody might still be inside. He rang the doorbell and, just to be sure, knocked as well. Barely had the door begun to open when he burst through it with a violence worthy of Catarella. The girl who had come to the door jumped back, terrified.

"What . . . what do you want? Please . . . please don't hurt me."

She was obviously convinced the man before her was a robber. She had turned deathly pale.

"I'm sorry if I frightened you," said Montalbano. "I have no reason to hurt you. Montalbano's the name."

"Oh, how silly of me," the girl said. "I remember you now. I saw you once on television. Please come in."

"Is Mr. Carlentini here?" the inspector asked, following her inside.

"You haven't heard?"

"Haven't heard what?" said Montalbano, becoming even more distressed.

"Poor Mr. Carlentini —"

"Is dead?" Montalbano howled, as if she'd just informed him that the person he loved most in the world had died.

The girl looked at him with mild stupefaction.

"No, he isn't dead. He had a stroke. He's recovering."

"But can he speak? Can he remember things?"

"Of course."

"How can I talk to him?"

"Now?"

"Now."

The girl glanced at her watch.

"Maybe there's still time. He's at Santa Maria Hospital in Montelusa."

She went into a room full of papers, folders, dossiers, and binders, dialed a number, and asked for Room 114. Then she said:

"Giulio —" But she interrupted herself. It was a well-known fact that the notary never let a pretty one get away. And the young woman on the phone was thirtyish and tall, with long black hair down to the small of her back and beautiful legs.

"Mr. Carlentini," she continued. "Inspector Montalbano's here at the office and would like to speak with you. . . . Okay? I'll talk to you later."

She handed the phone to Montalbano and discreetly left the room.

"Hello, Mr. Carlentini? Montalbano here. I just wanted a little information from you. Do you remember, a few years back, I turned over to you a passbook account for five hundred million lire. . . . ? Oh, so you do remember? I'm asking you because I was worried you might have invested the money with Mr. Gargano's firm and so. . . . No, no, please don't be offended. . . . no, of course not, I didn't mean. . . . As you can imagine, I . . . Okay,

56

okay, I'm very sorry. And get well soon."

He hung up. The notary, at the mere mention of Gargano's name, had taken offense.

"Do you think I would be so stupid as to trust in a crook like Gargano?" he had said.

François's money was safe.

Still, as he was getting in his car to go to the station, Montalbano swore he would make *ragioniere* Gargano pay, dearly and in full, for the terrible fright he'd given him.

4

But he never made it to the station, for on the way there he determined he'd had a rough day and therefore deserved a consolation prize. He'd heard vague mention of a trattoria that had opened a few months back about ten kilometers past Montelusa, off the provincial road to Giardina, where the food was supposed to be good. He even remembered the name, *Giugiù 'u Carrittèri,* that is, "Giugiù the Carter." After failing four times to find the right road, and at the very moment he'd decided to turn back and put in yet another appearance at the Trattoria San Calogero — since meanwhile he was getting more and more ravenous — he saw in the beam of the headlights a sign for the restaurant, a hand-painted piece of wood attached to a lamppost. After five minutes of authentic dirt road of the sort that no longer exists — all pits and rocks — he finally arrived, though for a moment he suspected it might all be a hoax on the part of Giugiù, who was probably only pretending to be a carter when he was actually a rally race car driver. Still feeling suspicious, he was hardly convinced by the secluded little white house he came to. Poorly whitewashed and with no neon sign, it consisted of a single, ground-floor room with another room on top. A dim, depressing light filtered out through the two windows on the bottom floor. Surely the final touch on the hoax. There were two cars in the parking area. He got out and hesitated, feeling indecisive. He didn't want the evening to end with food poisoning. He tried to remember who it was that had recommended the place to him, and it finally came back to him: Assistant Inspector Lindt, the son of a Swiss couple ("Any relation to the chocolate?" he'd asked when they were introduced), who until six months ago had worked in Bolzano.

"That guy probably can't tell a chicken from a salmon!" he said to himself.

But at that moment, borne ever so lightly on the evening breeze, an aroma reached his nostrils and opened them up; it was a scent of genuine, savory cooking, of dishes cooked the way the Lord intended them to be. His misgivings dispelled, he opened the door and went inside. There were eight small tables in the room, one of which was taken by a middle-aged couple. He sat down at the first table he came upon.

"I'm sorry, but that one's reserved," said the waiter and owner, a bald, sixtyish man, tall and paunchy, with a handlebar mustache.

Obediently, the inspector stood back up. He was about to set his buttocks down at the next table when the man with the mustache spoke again.

"That one too."

Montalbano began to feel irritated. Was this guy jerking him around or something? Was he trying to pick a fight?

"They're all reserved. If you want, I can set a place for you here," the waiter-owner said, seeing the troubled look in his customer's eyes.

He was pointing to a tiny little sideboard covered with cutlery, glasses, and dishes, very near the kitchen door, through which wafted that aroma that sated you before you'd even begun eating.

"That'd be great," said the inspector.

He found himself sitting as if in the corner at school, with the wall practically in his face. To view the room he would have had to sit sideways in the chair and twist his neck halfway around. But what the hell did he care about viewing the room?

"If you feel up to it, I've got burning *pirciati* tonight," said the man with the mustache.

Montalbano was familiar with *pirciati,* a kind of pasta, but wondered what the "burning" referred to. He didn't want to give the man the satisfaction of being asked how the *pirciati* were cooked, so he limited himself to a single question:

"What do you mean, 'If I feel up to it'?"

"Exactly what I said: 'If you feel up to it,'" was his reply.

"Oh, I feel up to it, don't you worry about that."

The man shrugged, disappeared into the kitchen, then returned a few minutes later and started eyeing the inspector. The other couple in the room called him over and asked for the bill. The man with the mustache brought it, and they paid and left without saying good-bye.

Saying hello and good-bye must not be the rule around here, thought Montalbano, remembering that he himself, upon entering, did not say hello to anyone.

The man with the mustache came out of the kitchen and assumed the exact same pose as before.

"It'll be ready in five minutes," he said. "Want me to turn on the television while you're waiting?"

"No."

Finally, a woman's voice called out from the kitchen.

"Giugiù!"

The *pirciati* arrived. They smelled like heaven on earth. The man with the mustache leaned against the doorjamb as though settling in to witness a performance.

Montalbano decided to let the aroma penetrate all the way to the bottom of his lungs.

As he was greedily inhaling, the man spoke.

"Want a bottle of wine within reach before you begin eating?"

The inspector nodded yes; he didn't feel like talking. A one-liter jug of very dense red wine was set before him. Montalbano poured out a glass of it and put the first bite in his mouth. He choked, coughed, and tears came to his eyes. He had the unmistakable impression that his taste buds had caught fire. In a single draft he emptied the glass of wine, which didn't kid around as to its alcohol content.

"Go at it nice and easy," the waiter-owner said.

"But what's in it?" asked Montalbano, still half choking.

"Olive oil, half an onion, two cloves of

garlic, two salted anchovies, a teaspoon of fine capers, black olives, tomatoes, basil, half a pimento, salt, Pecorino cheese, and black pepper," the man ran down the list with a hint of sadism in his voice.

"Jesus," said Montalbano. "And who's in the kitchen?"

"My wife," said the man with the mustache, going to the door to greet three new customers.

Punctuating his forkfuls with gulps of wine and alternating groans of extreme agony and unbearable pleasure (*Is there such a thing as extreme cuisine, like extreme sex?* he wondered at one point), Montalbano even had the courage to soak up the sauce left in the bottom of the bowl with his bread, periodically wiping away the beads of sweat that were forming on his brow.

"And what would you like for a second course, sir?"

The inspector understood that with that "sir," the owner was paying him military honors.

"Nothing."

"You're right. The problem with burning *pirciati* is that you don't get your taste buds back till the next day."

Montalbano asked for the bill, payed a

pittance, got up, headed toward the door and, in accordance with local custom, did not say good-bye. Right beside the exit he noticed a large photograph, and under it the following words:

MILLION LIRE REWARD TO ANYONE WITH INFORMATION ON THIS MAN.

"Who is he?" he asked, turning to the man with the mustache.

"You don't know him? That's that god-damn son of a bitch of a broker, Emanuele Gargano, the man who —"

"Why do you want information on him?"

"So I can catch him and cut his throat."

"What did he do to you?"

"To me, nothing. But he stole thirty million lire from my wife."

"Tell the lady she shall have her revenge," the inspector said solemnly, putting his hand over his heart.

He realized he was totally drunk.

The moon in the sky was frightening, so much did it seem like daylight outside. Montalbano drove down the road giddily, thinking he could handle it, screeching around the curves, taking his speed alternately down to ten and up to a hundred kilometers an hour. Halfway between Montelusa and Vigàta he saw the billboard behind which lay hidden the little road that led to the dilapidated cottage with the great Saracen olive tree beside it. Since over his last three kilometers he'd barely avoided crashing head-on into two different cars coming in the opposite direction, he decided to turn down this road and sit out his drunkenness under the branches of that tree, which he hadn't been to visit for almost a year.

As he bore right to turn onto the little road, he immediately had the impression he'd made a mistake, since in the place of the narrow country road there was now a broad band of asphalt. Maybe he'd confused one billboard with another. He put the car in reverse and ended up backing into one of the supports of the billboard, which began to teeter dangerously. FERRAGUTO FURNITURE — MONTELUSA, it read. No doubt about it, that was the right sign. He drove back out onto the road and after going about a hundred yards he found himself in front of the gate to a small villa that had just been built. The little rustic cottage was gone, the Saracen olive tree too. He felt disoriented. He recognized nothing in a landscape that had once been so familiar to him.

Was it possible that one liter of wine, no matter how strong, could reduce him to such a state? He got out of the car and, as he was pissing, kept turning his head to look around. The moonlight afforded good visibility, but what he saw looked alien to him. He took a flashlight out of the glove compartment and proceeded to circle round the enclosure. The house was finished but clearly not inhabited; the windowpanes still had protective Xs of masking tape over them. The garden inside the enclosure was fairly large. They were building some sort of gazebo there; he could see a pile of tools nearby. Shovels, pickaxes, cement troughs. When he got to the area behind the house, he stumbled into what at first seemed to him a bush of buckthorn. He pointed the flashlight, got a better look, and cried out. He'd seen death. Or, rather, the threshold of death. The great Saracen olive tree lay before him, moribund, having been felled and up-rooted. It was dying. They had cut the branches from the trunk with an electric saw, and the trunk itself had been deeply wounded by an ax. The leaves had withered and were drying up. In his confusion

66

Montalbano realized he was weeping, sniffing up the mucus that kept dripping out of his nose, breathing in starts the way little children do. He reached out and placed his hand over the space of a particularly wide gash. Under his palm he could still feel a slight dampness from the sap; it was oozing out little by little, like the blood of a man slowly bleeding to death. He lifted his hand from the wound and tore off a few leaves, which still resisted. He put them in his pocket. Then his tears gave way to a kind of lucid, controlled rage.

He went back to his car, took off his jacket, put the flashlight into his pants pocket, turned on the high beam of the headlights, and confronted the cast-iron gate, scaling it like a monkey, no doubt thanks to the wine, whose effect hadn't yet worn off. With a leap worthy of Tarzan, he found himself inside a garden with graveled paths all around, carved stone benches every ten yards or so, clay pots with plants, faux-Roman amphorae with faux-marine excrescences, and capitaled columns clearly made just down the road in Fiacca. And the inevitable, complex, ultramodern barbecue grill. He headed towards the unfinished gazebo, rummaged through the tools, selected a sledgehammer, seized the handle with a firm grip, and began to shatter the ground-floor windows, of which there were two on each side of the house.

After demolishing six windowpanes, he turned the corner and immediately saw a group of motionless, quasi-human figures. Oh God, what were they? He pulled the flashlight out of his pocket and turned it on. They were eight large statues, temporarily bunched together until they could be arranged by the house's owner according to his liking. Snow White and the Seven Dwarfs.

"Wait there, I'll be right back," Montalbano said to them.

He carefully pulverized the two remaining windows, and then, twirling the sledgehammer high over his head — just as Orlando in fury had done with his sword — he let loose on the group of statues, swinging blindly in every direction.

In some ten minutes' time, all that was left of Snow White, Happy, Grumpy, Dumpy, Sleazy, Snoopy, Duck, and Bumful, or whatever the hell they were called, was a litter of tiny colored fragments. Montalbano, however, still didn't feel satisfied. Also near the unfinished gazebo, he discovered some cans of spray paint. Picking up the green, he wrote the word ASSHOLE four times in big block letters, once on each side of the house. After which he rescaled the front gate, got back in his car, and drove home to Marinella, now feeling completely sober again.

Back home in Marinella, he spent half the night putting his house back in order after the havoc he'd created looking for the notary's receipt. Not that it really need have taken all that time, but the fact is, when you empty out all your drawers you find a great many old, forgotten papers, some of which demand, almost by force, to be read, and you inevitably end up plunging deeper and deeper into the vortex of memory, as things that for years upon years you'd done all in your power to forget begin to come back to you. It's a wicked game, memory, one that you always end up losing.

He went to bed around three in the morning. But after getting up at least three times to drink a glass of water, he decided to bring a pitcher into the bedroom, setting it on the nightstand. Result: By seven o'clock his belly was as though pregnant with water. It was a cloudy morning, and this increased his nervous agitation, which was already at the high-water mark from his bad night. The telephone rang. He picked up the receiver with determination.

"Don't be breaking my balls, Cat."

"Is not who you tink, signore, is me."

"And who are you?"

"Don' you rec'nize me, signore? Is Adelina."

"Adelina! What's the matter?"

"Signore, I wanted a tell you I can't come today."

"That's okay, don't —"

"An' I can't come tomorrow neither, an'a day after that neither."

"What's wrong?"

"My younges' son's wife was rush to the hospital with a bad bellyache and I gotta look after 'er kids. There's four of 'em and the oldest is ten and he's a bigger rascal than 'is dad."

"It's okay, Adelina, don't worry about it."

He hung up, went into the bathroom, grabbed a small mountain of dirty laundry, including the sweater that Livia had given him, the one all caked with sand, and threw everything into the washer. Unable to find a clean shirt, he put on the same one he'd worn the previous day. He thought he'd have to eat out for at least three lunches and three dinners, but he swore to himself he would resist temptation and remain faithful to the San Calogero. Thanks to Adelina's phone call, however, his bad mood was now overflowing, convinced as he was of his inability to take care of himself or his house.

At the station there seemed to be dead calm. Catarella didn't even notice his arrival, involved as he was in a phone conversation that must have been rather trying, since from time to time he would wipe his brow with his sleeve. On his desk he found a scrap of paper with two names on it, Giacomo Pellegrino and Michela Manganaro, and two corresponding telephone numbers. He recognized Mimì's handwriting and immediately remembered that these were the names of the employees of King Midas Associates, along with, of course, Mariastella Cosentino. Mimì, however, hadn't added their addresses, and the inspector preferred to talk to people face-to-face.

"Mimì," he called.

Nobody came. The guy was probably still in bed or drinking his first cup of coffee.

"Fazio!"

Fazio showed up at once.

"Isn't Inspector Augello here?"

"He's not coming in today, Chief, and not tomorrow or the next day, either."

Just like his housekeeper, Adelina. Did Mimì likewise have grandchildren to look after?

"And why not?"

"What do you mean, why not, Chief? Have you forgotten? He's on marriage leave, starting today."

It had completely slipped the inspector's mind. And to think it was he who'd introduced Mimì — even if it was, in a sense, for unmentionable reasons — to his future wife, Beatrice, a fine, beautiful girl.

"So when's he getting married?"

"In five days. And don't forget, 'cause you're supposed to be Inspector Augello's witness."

"I won't forget. Listen, are you busy?"

"I'll be with you in a second. There's some guy here, Giacomo Pellegrino, who came in to report some acts of vandalism against a small villa he just now finished building."

"When did this happen?"

"Last night."

"Okay, take care of it and come back."

So he, Montalbano, was the vandal.

Hearing his exploits described that way, here, inside the police station, he felt a little ashamed of himself. But how could he ever set it right? He couldn't very well go over to Fazio's room and say: "Listen, Mr. Pellegrino, I'm very sorry, I'm the one who —"

He stopped. Giacomo Pellegrino, Fazio had said. That was one of the names Mimì had written down with the phone number on the piece of paper in front of him. He quickly committed Pellegrino's phone number to memory, got up, and went into Fazio's office.

His sergeant, who was writing something down, glanced up at Montalbano. They barely looked at each other, but they understood. Fazio kept writing. What was it Mimì had said about Giacomo Pellegrino? That he was a young guy, a graduate in business economics. The man sitting in front of Fazio's desk looked like a shepherd and must have been at least sixty. Fazio finished writing, and then Pellegrino, with some difficulty, signed the paper. Business economics, my eye. This guy'd never got out of third grade. Fazio took the report back from him, and at this point the inspector intervened.

"Did you leave your telephone number?" Montalbano asked.

"No," said the man.

"Well, it's always better to have it. What is it?"

The man dictated it to Fazio, who wrote it down. It wasn't the same. It seemed more like a number from the Montereale area.

"Are you from around here, Mr. Pellegrino?"

"No, I've got a house near Montereale."

"So why did you have a house built between Vigàta and Montelusa?"

He'd just put his foot deep in his mouth, and he realized this at once. Fazio hadn't told him where the villa was located. And indeed the sergeant began staring at the inspector, his eyes narrowing to tiny little slits. But Pellegrino probably thought the two cops had already discussed things when Fazio was called out of the room; he did not seem surprised by the question.

"It's not mine. It belongs to my nephew, one of my brother's boys. He's got the same name as me."

"Ah!" said Montalbano, feigning astonishment. "Now I get it. Your nephew's the young man who worked for King Midas Associates, right?"

"Yessir, that's him."

"I'm sorry, but why are you reporting

74

the crime instead of your nephew, who's the owner?"

"Mr. Pellegrino has power of attorney," Fazio cut in.

"I guess your nephew works too much and can't look after —"

"No," said the man. "I'll tell you what happened. About a month ago, on the same morning that son of a bitch Gargano was supposed to come back —"

"What, did he take your money too?"

"Yessir, he did, everything I owned. The morning before that, my nephew came out to Montereale to tell me Gargano'd called him and ordered him to go to Germany for some business. His plane was leaving from Palermo at four in the afternoon. My nephew told me he'd be away for at least a month and asked me to look after the construction. He should be back any day now."

"So if I need to talk to him I won't find him in Vigàta?"

"No sir."

"Do you have an address or a phone number in Germany where I can reach your nephew?"

"Are you kidding?"

5

Why was it that ever since Garzullo the land surveyor, rest his soul, came into the Vigàta office of King Midas, revolver in hand, threatening to commit a massacre, the inspector couldn't make a move without running into someone or something connected in one way or another to *ragioniere* Gargano? As he was contemplating this string of coincidences of the sort that one finds both in second-rate detective novels and in the tritest everyday reality, Fazio came in.

"Awaiting your orders, Chief. But please explain one thing for me first. How did you know where Pellegrino's villa was? I never told you. Care to tell me, for curiosity's sake?"

"No."

Fazio threw his hands up. The inspector had decided to play it safe. With Fazio, it was better to be cautious. The guy was a true cop.

"And I also know that they broke all the windows on the ground floor, smashed

Snow White and the Seven Dwarfs to dust, and wrote 'asshole' on all four walls," the inspector added. "Am I right?"

"You're right. They used a sledge-hammer and a can of green spray paint they found at the house."

"Terrific. So what do you make of that? Think I talk to spirits? Have a crystal ball? Have magical powers?" asked Montalbano, getting more and more enraged with each question.

"No sir. But there's no need to get angry."

"But of course I get angry! I drove by there this morning. I wanted to see how the olive tree was doing."

"Was it doing well?" Fazio asked with a hint of irony. He knew about the tree as well as the rock on the jetty, the two places where his boss sometimes sought refuge.

"It's not there anymore. They chopped it down to make room for the house."

Fazio turned very serious, as though Montalbano had just informed him of the death of someone very dear to him.

"I understand," he said softly.

"You understand what?"

"Nothing. Got any orders to give me?"

"Yes. Now that we know that Giacomo Pellegrino is living it up in Germany, I'd like you to find me the address of this Miss or Mrs. Michela Manganaro who worked for Gargano."

"I'll have it for you in a minute. Want me to go first to Brucale's and buy you a new shirt?"

"Yeah, thanks, and get me three while you're at it. But how'd you guess I needed shirts? Now you're the one with magical powers who talks to spirits!"

"No need to talk to spirits, Chief. I can see you didn't change your shirt this morning, and you really should have, 'cause one of the cuffs is stained with dried paint. Green paint," he emphasized with a little smile, going out.

Miss Michela Manganaro lived with her parents in a ten-story public housing unit near the cemetery. Montalbano thought it best not to forewarn her of his coming, either by telephone or even via the intercom. He'd just finished parking the car when he saw a man coming out the main door.

"Excuse me, could you tell me what floor the Manganaros live on?"

"Fifth floor, damn it all!"

"What have you got against the Manganaros?"

"For a week now the elevators only go

up to the fifth floor. And I live on the tenth! I have to climb those stairs twice a day! They've always been lucky bastards, those Manganaros. Just imagine, a few years ago they even won the numbers!"

"Did they win much?"

"Small potatoes. But can you imagine the self-satisfaction?"

Montalbano went into the elevator and pressed the button for the fifth floor. The elevator went up and stopped at the third floor. He tried everything, but the thing wouldn't budge. Forced to climb up two flights of stairs, he consoled himself with the thought that at least he'd been spared the other three.

"Whoozat?" an elderly woman's voice called out from behind the door.

"Montalbano's the name. I'm a police inspector."

"What do you want from us?"

"I need to talk to your daughter Michela. Is she at home?"

"Yes, but she's lying down. Got a touch of the flu. Wait just a minute while I call my husband."

There followed a shout that momentarily startled Montalbano.

"Filì! Com'ere! There's some guy here says he's a police inspector!"

79

Apparently he hadn't succeeded in convincing the lady, to judge by that "says."

Then, still behind the locked door, the woman said:

"Talk loud 'cause my husband's deaf!"

"Whoozat?" said a man's voice this time, sounding irritated.

"I'm with the police, open up!"

He'd yelled so loudly that, even as the Manganaros' door remained stubbornly closed, the other two doors on the landing opened, and two spectators, one at each door, appeared: a little girl of about ten who was eating a morning snack, and a man of about fifty in a sleeveless undershirt with a patch over his left eye.

"Speak louder, Manganaro's deaf," was the friendly advice of the man in the undershirt.

Even louder? He did a few breathing exercises to ventilate his lungs, as he'd once seen a champion underwater diver do, and, having stored as much air as possible, he yelled:

"Police!"

He heard doors open simultaneously on the floors above and below, as some agitated voices began to ask:

"What's going on? What's happening?"

The door to the Manganaro flat opened

very very slowly, and then a parrot appeared. Or that, at least, was the inspector's first impression. Long, yellow nose, purple cheeks, big, dark eyes, loud green shirt, and a tiny crest of red hair on his head.

"Come in," the parrot muttered. "But please be quiet, my daughter's asleep. She doesn't feel so good."

He showed the inspector into an incongruously Swedish-looking living room. Perched on a stand was Mr. Manganaro's twin brother, who at least had the honesty to remain a bird and not pass himself off as a man. Manganaro's wife, a kind of injured sparrow accidentally or maliciously riddled with buckshot who dragged her left leg, entered the room carrying with difficulty a tiny tray with a demitasse of coffee.

"It's already got sugar," she said, sitting down and making herself comfortable on the little sofa.

It was obvious her curiosity was eating her alive. She probably didn't have many opportunities to amuse herself, and she was settling in to enjoy this one.

Seeing how things are, thought *Montalbano, what kind of daughter-bird is going to come from a cross between a parrot and a sparrow?*

"I informed Michela. She's getting up and will be right in," twittered the sparrow.

But where did she dredge up that voice she called her husband with? Montalbano wondered. Then he remembered reading in a travel book about certain tiny birds that could wail like sirens. The lady must belong to that species.

The coffee had so much sugar in it that the inspector's mouth turned sticky. The first to speak was the parrot, the one disguised as a man.

"I know why you wanna talk to my daughter. 'Cause of that goddamn son of a bitch Gargano. Am I right?"

"Yes," yelled Montalbano. "Were you also a victim of Gargano's sch—"

"Nahhh!" said the man, violently thrusting his right arm forward and clapping his left hand into the hollow of the elbow.

"Filì!" his wife scolded him, using her second voice, the one from the Last Judgment.

The windowpanes made a tinkling noise.

"Do you think Filippo Manganaro would be so stupid as to fall for Gargano's little shell game? You know, I didn't even want my daughter to go work for that swindler!"

"You knew Gargano before all this?"

"No, but I didn't need to know him 'cause they're all swindlers: the banks, bankers, stock marketeers, everybody who works with money. They can't help it, man, it's the way things are. If you want, I'll explain it to you. You by any chance ever read a book called *Capital*, by Marx?"

"Parts of it," said Montalbano. "Are you a Communist?"

"Hit it, Turì!"

The inspector, not understanding his reply, looked at him dumbfounded. Who was this Turì? He found out a moment later, when the man's twin, the real parrot, whose name was apparently Turiddru, cleared his throat and started singing the "Internationale." He sang it rather well, and Montalbano began to feel a wave of nostalgia well up inside him. He was about to compliment the bird's teacher when Michela appeared in the doorway. At the sight of her, Montalbano's jaw dropped. The last thing he expected was this strapping, rather tall brunette with violet eyes, beautiful and full of life, nose slightly reddened from the flu, wearing a miniskirt halfway up her slightly but perfectly plump thighs and a white blouse that barely contained a pair of full breasts imprisoned by no bra. A quick, wicked thought, like a viper darting through the grass, flashed into his mind. No question but that the handsome Gargano had wet his whistle, or tried to, with a girl like her.

"Okay, I'm available now."

Available? She said it with a deep, slightly gravelly voice, Marlene Dietrich–style, which made Montalbano so hot and bothered that he could barely restrain himself from crowing like the professor in *The Blue Angel*. The girl sat down, pulling her skirt as much as possible towards her knees, looking demure, eyes downcast, one hand on her leg and the other on the armrest. It was the pose of a good girl from an honest, hardworking family. The inspector recovered the power of speech.

"I'm sorry to make you get out of bed."

"Don't worry about it."

"I'm here to ask you for some information on *ragioniere* Gargano and the agency where you used to work."

"Go ahead. But you should know I was already questioned by someone from your office. Inspector Augello, if I'm not mistaken. Although I must say, frankly, he seemed more interested in other things."

"Other things?"

He regretted his question even as he was

asking it. He'd understood what she meant. And he imagined the scene in his mind: Mimì asking question after question, as his eyes, meanwhile, were delicately removing her blouse, bra (if she was wearing one that day), skirt, and panties. No way Mimì could have resisted, face-to-face with a beauty like this one. He thought of Mimì's future wife, Beatrice, and how many bitter pills the poor thing would have to swallow.

The girl didn't answer the question; she knew that the inspector had understood. And she smiled. Or, rather, she gave one to imagine she was smiling, as she kept her head bowed, as was only proper in the company of a stranger. The parrot and the sparrow contemplated their baby with satisfaction.

At this point the girl raised her violet eyes and looked at Montalbano as though awaiting his questions. But in reality she was telling him something, quite clearly, without using any words:

Don't waste your time here, she was saying. *I can't talk. Wait for me downstairs.*

Message received, Montalbano's eyes replied.

The inspector decided not to waste any more time. He pretended to be surprised and put out.

"So you really were already interrogated? And it was all put on the record?"

"Of course."

"But why haven't I seen anything?"

"Don't ask me. Ask Inspector Augello, who, aside from being totally conceited, is losing his head these days because he's getting married."

And then there was light. What alerted him were the words "totally conceited," which, in the presence of her old-fashioned parents, were definitely standing in for the word "asshole," far more pregnant in meaning, as literary critics used to say. But absolute certainty came immediately after that. The girl had surely granted her favors (as one says in the presence of old-fashioned parents) and Mimì, having lain with the aforesaid girl, had then disposed of her by revealing that he was engaged to be soon married.

He stood up. They all stood up.

"I'm terribly sorry," he said.

They were all very understanding.

"These things happen," said the parrot.

A small procession formed, with the girl at the head, the inspector next, then the father and behind him the mother. Watching the undulant movement in front of him, Montalbano felt green with envy towards

Mimì. After opening the door, the girl extended her hand to him.

"Pleased to have met you," she said with her mouth. But her eyes said: *Wait for me.*

He waited a little more than half an hour, the time Michela needed to doll herself up properly and get rid of the redness around her cute little nose. Montalbano saw her appear in the doorway and look around, whereupon he gave a light toot of the horn and opened the car door. The girl walked towards the car with an air of indifference, at a slow pace, but once she'd reached the car she hopped in quickly, shut the door, and said:

"Let's get out of here."

Montalbano, who managed at that moment to notice that Michela had forgotten to put on a bra, put the car in gear and drove off.

"I had to put up a fight. My parents didn't want to let me go out; they're worried I'll have a relapse," the girl said. Then she asked: "Where should we go to talk?"

"You want to go to the police station?"

"And what if I run into that asshole?"

Thus were Montalbano's worst (and best) suspicions confirmed in a single stroke.

"Anyway, I don't like police stations," Michela added.

"How about a café?"

"Are you kidding? People gossip too much about me as it is. Although with you, I guess, there wouldn't be any danger of that."

"Why not?"

"Because you're old enough to be my father."

It would have been better if she'd stabbed him. The car swerved slightly.

"Down and out for the count," said the girl by way of commentary. "It's a strategy that often works to deflate ambitious old geezers. But it depends how you say it."

Then she repeated it in an even deeper, more gravelly voice:

"You're old enough to be my father."

She'd managed to instill her voice with a heady savor of taboo and incest.

Montalbano couldn't help but imagine her next to him in bed, naked, sweaty, and panting. This girl was dangerous. Not just beautiful, but a bitch.

"So, where are we going?" he asked in an authoritarian tone.

"Where do you live?"

"There are people at my place."

"Married?"

"No. Come on, are you going to make up your mind?"

"I think I know a place," Michela said. "Take the second road on the right."

The inspector quickly turned onto the second road on the right. It was one of those rare roads that still tell you immediately where they're going to take you: out into the open country. And they tell you this by means of houses that grow smaller and smaller until they turn into little more than dice with a little patch of green around them; or by means of lampposts and telephone poles that suddenly no longer line up straight; or by means of the road surface, which suddenly begins to give way to grass. Finally even the white dice disappear.

"Should I keep going?"

"Yes. Soon you'll see a dirt road on your left. But don't worry about your car, it's well maintained."

Montalbano turned onto the road and soon found himself in the middle of a kind of dense wood of monkey puzzle trees and clumps of weeds.

"There's nobody here today," said the girl, "because it's a weekday. You should see all the traffic on Saturdays and Sundays!"

"You come here often?"

"When I happen to."

Montalbano rolled down the window and took out a pack of cigarettes.

"Do you mind . . . ?"

"No. Let me have one too."

They smoked in silence. Halfway through his cigarette, the inspector started in.

"All right, I'd like to get a better idea about how Gargano's system worked."

"Make your questions specific."

"Where did you guys keep the money Gargano stole?"

"Well, sometimes it was Gargano who would come in with the checks, and then either me or Mariastella or Giacomo would deposit them at the local branch of the Cassa di Credito. We'd do the same when the client came directly to the office. Some time after that, Gargano started having the sums credited to his bank in Bologna. But the money didn't stay there very long, either, as far as we knew. Apparently it ended up in places like Switzerland and Liechtenstein, I don't know."

"Why'd he send it there?"

"What a question! Because he was investing it, so it would earn more money. At least that's what we thought."

"And what do you think now?"

"That he was piling up all the cash abroad so he could screw everybody when the time was right."

"Were you also . . ."

"Screwed by him? No, I never gave him a cent. I couldn't, even if I'd wanted to. You met my dad. He did manage to screw us out of two months' salary, however."

"Listen, do you mind if I ask you a personal question?"

"Come on!"

"Did Gargano ever try to sleep with you?"

Michela burst into sudden, uncontrollable laughter, her violet eyes turning brighter as they began to sparkle with tears. Montalbano let her get it out of her system, wondering what was so funny about the question. Michela got hold of herself.

"Officially, he was courting me. But he was also courting poor Mariastella, who was really jealous of me. You know, chocolates, flowers, that kind of thing. . . . But if I'd ever told him I wanted to sleep with him, you know what would have happened?"

"No, tell me."

"He would have fainted. Gargano's gay."

6

The inspector looked stunned. This was something that had never even crossed his mind. But after recovering from his initial shock, he thought about it: Was the fact that Gargano was homosexual of any importance to the investigation? Maybe yes and maybe no. Mimì, however, had said nothing about it to him.

"Are you sure? Did he tell you himself?"

"I'm more than sure, even though he never mentioned it to me. It was clear from the start, the first time we ever looked at each other."

"Did you point out this . . . this fact, or, rather, this impression of yours, to Inspector Augello?"

"Augello asked me certain questions with his mouth, but his eyes were asking something else. To be honest, I can't really remember if I talked about it with that asshole or not."

"Excuse me, but why are you so down on Augello?"

"Well, you see, Inspector, I slept with

Augello, because I liked him. But before I left his house, he, with a towel over his dick, let me know that he was engaged and about to get married. Who the hell asked? He was so lame that I regretted ever sleeping with him. There you have it. I'd like to forget about him."

"Was Miss Cosentino aware that Gargano —"

"Look, Inspector, even if Gargano had suddenly turned into some horrible monster — say, Kafka's cockroach — she would have continued to worship him, lost in her loving raptures, and not noticed a thing. Anyway, I don't think poor Mariastella can really tell the difference between a rooster and a hen."

She certainly was full of surprises, this Michela Manganaro. So now she was pulling out Kafka's *Metamorphosis*?

"You like him?"

"Who, Gargano?"

"No, Kafka."

"I've read everything from *The Trial* to the *Letters to Milena*. Are we here to talk about literature?"

Montalbano absorbed the blow.

"And what about Giacomo Pellegrino?"

"Giacomo understood right away, of course, maybe even before I did. Because

Giacomo's also gay. And before you ask me, I can tell you I also mentioned this to Augello."

Him too? And he understood right away? The inspector wanted confirmation.

"Him too?" he asked.

The question came out with an intonation typical of a Sicilian comic, half shocked, half annoyed. He felt immediately embarrassed, because that wasn't remotely his intention.

"Him too," Michela said with no intonation whatsoever.

"It's possible," Montalbano began cautiously, as though walking through a field of antipersonnel mines, ". . . but it's purely a hypothesis, I should point out . . . that Giacomo and Gargano might have had a relationship that could be termed somewhat —"

"Why are you talking like that?" said the girl, opening wide her beautiful violet eyes.

"I'm sorry," said the inspector, "I'm a little confused. I meant to say —"

"I understood perfectly well what you meant to say. And the answer is: maybe yes, maybe no."

"Have you read that one too?"

"No. I don't like D'Annunzio. But if I were to make my own hypothesis, as you call it, I would lean more towards the 'yes' than the 'no.' "

"What makes you say that?"

"Something, in my opinion, started between the two almost immediately. They would sometimes stand apart and whisper . . ."

"But that doesn't mean anything. They might have been talking business."

"And looking into each other's eyes that way? And then there were the 'yes' days and the 'no' days."

"I don't know what you mean."

"You know, it's typical of lovers. If their last encounter went well, then the next time they see each other they're all smiles and touchy-feely . . . But if things didn't go well, if they'd had a quarrel, then there's a kind of chill, they avoid touching each other, looking each other in the eye. Gargano, whenever he came to Vigàta, would stay at least a week, and so there was plenty of time for 'yes' days and 'no' days. It would have been hard for me not to notice."

"Do you have any idea where they would meet?"

"No. Gargano was a very private man. And Giacomo was also really reserved."

"Listen, after Gargano disappeared, did

you ever hear from him again? Did he write or phone the office or make any kind of contact?"

"You shouldn't be asking *me* that; you should be asking Mariastella. She's the only one left at the office. I never went back after I realized that some infuriated client might take things out on me. Giacomo was the smartest of all of us, since the morning Gargano didn't come in, he didn't show up either. He must have had an inkling."

"An inkling of what?"

"That Gargano'd made off with all the money. You see, Inspector, Giacomo was the only one of us who understood anything about Gargano's business dealings. He probably went to the bank the day before and found out that no funds had been transferred from Bologna to Vigàta. At which point he would have realized something wasn't right, so he stayed away. At least that's what I thought."

"And you were wrong, because the day before Gargano arrived, Giacomo left for Germany."

"Really?" said the girl, genuinely astonished. "To do what?"

"Sent there on assignment by Gargano. For a stay of at least one month. To take care of some business."

"And who told you that?"

"Giacomo's uncle. The one looking after the construction of the house."

"What house?" asked Michela, completely confused.

"You didn't know Giacomo was building a house just off the road between Vigàta and Montelusa?"

Michela put her head in her hands.

"What are you saying? Giacomo scraped by on his salary of two million two hundred thousand lire. That much I know for certain!"

"Maybe his parents —"

"His parents are from Vizzini and get by on the chicory in their garden. Listen, Inspector, this whole story you've just told me doesn't make any sense. It's true that every now and then Gargano used to send Giacomo off to clear up certain problems, but it was always unimportant stuff, and it always involved our own affiliates. I seriously doubt he would ever send him to Germany on important business. As I said, Giacomo knew more than the rest of us, but there was no way he could operate on an international level. He's not old enough, and secondly —"

"How old is he?" Montalbano interrupted.

"Twenty-five. And, secondly, he has no

experience. No, I'm convinced he pulled out that excuse with his uncle because he wanted to disappear for a while. He knew he couldn't handle all the infuriated clients."

"So he goes into hiding for a whole month?"

"Bah. I don't know what to think," said Michela. "Give me a cigarette."

Montalbano gave her one and lit it. The girl smoked it in short drags, without opening her mouth, visibly agitated. The inspector didn't feel like talking either, so he put his brain on automatic pilot.

When she'd finished smoking, Michela said in her Marlene voice (or was it Garbo dubbed?):

"Now I have a headache."

She tried to open the window but couldn't.

"Allow me. Now and then it gets stuck."

He leaned over the girl and realized too late that he'd made a mistake.

Michela's arms were suddenly wrapped around his shoulders. Montalbano's mouth opened in astonishment, and that was his second mistake. Michela's mouth over-whelmed his half-open one and began a sort of meticulous exploration thereof with her tongue. Montalbano momentarily succumbed, then got hold of himself and executed a painful unsticking maneuver.

"Behave."

"Yes, Daddy," she said with a glint of amusement deep in her violet eyes. He turned on the ignition, put the car in gear, and drove off.

But that "behave" had not been addressed to the girl. It was addressed to that part of his body which, upon solicitation, had not only promptly responded but actually intoned in a ringing voice the patriotic anthem that goes: *The tombs shall open, the dead shall rise. . . .*

"*Maria santissima,* Chief! What a scare I got! I'm still shaking all over, Chief! Look at my hand. See it trembling, see it?"

"I see it. What happened?"

"The c'mishner called poissonally in poisson and axed for you. I tole 'im you's momintarily absint an' as soon as you got back I'd a tell you he wants a talk t'you. But then he axed, the c'mishner did, to talk to the rankling officer."

"The ranking officer, Cat."

"Whatever is, is, Chief. All 'at matters is we unnastand each other. So I was saying as how Inspector Augello's matrimoniously engaged to be married soon an' so he's on leavings, an' you know what the c'mishner says to me then? He says: 'I don't give a damn.' Just like that, Chief! So I says, since Fazio ain't here neither, there ain't no rankling nobody. And then he axed me what my name is an' so I says Catarella. So then he says, 'Listen, Santarella,' and I wanna make a point and put 'im right, so I says, 'My name's Catarella.' And y'know what the c'mishner said then? He said: 'I don't give a damn what your name is.' Just like that. He was outside himself, the c'mishner was!"

"Cat, we're gonna be here all night at this rate. What'd he want?"

"He tole me to tell you you got twenty-four hours to give 'im the answer you're asposta give 'im."

The Italian mail permitting, the c'mishner would receive the pseudo-anonymous letter the next day. That would calm him down.

"Any other news?"

"Nuthin' at all, Chief."

"Where's everybody else?"

"Fazio went over to Via Lincoln for a brawl, Gallo's at the Sciacchitano store 'cause there was a little holdup there —"

"What do you mean, 'little'?"

"I mean the holder upper's a little boy, thirteen years old, with a gun as big as my arm. An' Galluzzo's at the place where they found a bomb this morning that never bombed, and Imbrò and Gramaglia went to —"

"Okay, okay," said Montalbano. "You were right, Cat. All quiet on the western front."

And as he went into his office, Catarella scratched his head.

"It's not too quiet in the Westerns I seen, Chief!"

On the inspector's desk, Fazio had left a four-foot stack of papers to be signed, with a little note on top saying: "Extremely urgent." Montalbano cursed the saints, knowing there was no getting around it.

When he was seated at his usual table in the Trattoria San Calogero, the owner, Calogero, came up to him with a conspiratorial air.

"We got *nunnatu* today, Inspector."

"But isn't it illegal to fish for them?"

"Yes it is, but every now and then we're allowed to catch one crate per boat."

"So why do you mention it as if it's some kind of secret plot?"

" 'Cause everybody wants 'em and I haven't got enough."

"How are you going to cook them? With lemon?"

"No, Inspector. The babies meet their maker in the frying pan, rolled into dumplings."

Montalbano had to wait a bit, but it was worth it. The flat, crispy dumplings were studded with hundreds of little black dots, the tiny eyes of the newborn fishlets. The inspector ate them as if participating in a sacred rite, knowing all the while he was ingesting something along the lines of a massacre. To punish himself, he decided not to eat anything else. Once outside the trattoria, as sometimes happened, the irksome voice of his conscience made itself heard.

To punish yourself, you say? What a hypocrite you are, Montalbano! Wasn't it rather because you were afraid you might get indigestion? Do you know how many dumplings you put away? Eighteen!

For one reason or another he went to the port and walked all the way out to the lighthouse, relishing the air of the sea.

"Fazio, in your opinion, how many ways are there to get to Sicily from the mainland?"

"Three, Chief. By car, by train, or by boat. Or on foot, if you want."

"Fazio, I don't like you when you try to be clever."

"I wasn't trying to be clever. During the last war my dad came all the way from Bolzano to Palermo on foot."

"Have we got Gargano's license plate number somewhere?"

Fazio looked at him in surprise.

"Wasn't Augello handling this case?"

"Well, now I'm handling it. Got a problem with that?"

"Why should I have a problem with it? I'm gonna go look through Inspector Augello's papers. Actually, I think I'll give him a ring. If he finds out I've been sticking my nose in his stuff, the guy's liable to shoot me. Did you sign those papers there? Yes? Then I'll take them off your hands and bring you some more."

"If you bring me any more papers to sign, I'll make you eat them one by one."

Arms full of files, Fazio stopped in the doorway and turned around.

"If I may say so, Inspector, you're wasting your time on Gargano. You want to know what I think?"

"No, but if you really must, go ahead."

"Jesus, have you got a chip on your shoulder today! What'd you do, have some food go down the wrong way?"

And he went out, indignant, without revealing what he thought about the

Gargano case. Barely five minutes had passed when the door flew open and slammed against the wall, a small piece of plaster falling to the ground. Catarella appeared, face invisible, hidden by a stack of documents over three feet high in his arms.

"Beg your pardon, Chief, had to push the door open with my foot 'cause my arms are full."

"Stop right there!"

Catarella froze.

"What have you got there?" the inspector asked.

"Papers you're sposta sign. Fazio just now give 'em to me."

"I'm going to count to three, and if you haven't disappeared I'm going to start shooting."

Catarella obeyed, walking backwards and moaning in terror. A little vendetta on the part of Fazio, who'd taken offense.

A good half hour passed without any sign of Fazio. Had he moved on to sabotage?

"Fazio!"

He came in, dead serious.

"Your orders, sir."

"Still haven't got over it? You're really taking it hard, eh?"

"What am I supposed to be taking so hard?"

"The fact that I didn't let you tell me what you thought about Gargano. It's all right, you can tell me."

"I don't want to anymore."

Was this the Vigàta Central Police Station or the Maria Montessori Kindergarten? If he gave him a red shell or a button with three holes would Fazio agree to talk in exchange? Better to get on with things.

"So, about that license plate."

"I'm unable to reach Inspector Augello, he doesn't even answer his cell phone."

"Go ahead and look in his files."

"You authorizing me?"

"That's right. Go."

"There's no need. I've got it right here, in my pocket."

He pulled out a little scrap of paper and handed it to Montalbano, who refused to take it.

"How'd you find it?"

"Looking through Augello's files."

Montalbano felt like slapping him around. When he put his mind to it, Fazio could give an invertebrate a nervous fit.

"Go back now and look through Augello's files some more. I want to know the exact day when everyone was expecting Gargano to return."

"Gargano was supposed to be here by the first of September," Fazio said immediately. "There were dividends to pay. By nine in the morning there were already some twenty people waiting for him."

Montalbano realized that during the half hour in which Fazio had disappeared he was engrossed in Augello's papers. The man was a real cop and by now knew everything about the case.

"Why did they line up like that? Did he pay in cash?"

"No, Chief. He paid by check, wire, credit transfer, and so on. The ones who lined up to wait for him were the old retirees, who got a kick out of receiving their checks personally from him."

"Today's the fifth of October. That means he hasn't been heard from for thirty-five days."

"No, Chief. The secretary in Bologna said the last time she'd seen him was on the twenty-eighth of August. On that occasion Gargano told her that the following day — that is, the twenty-ninth — he'd be leaving to come down here. Since there are thirty-one days in August, *ragioniere* Gargano hasn't been seen for thirty-eight days."

The inspector looked at his watch, picked up the phone, and dialed a number.

"Hello?"

From her deserted office, Mariastella Cosentino had answered on the first ring, her voice filled with hope. Surely she was dreaming that one day the telephone would ring, and at the other end would be the warm, seductive voice of her beloved boss.

"Montalbano here."

"Oh."

The old girl's disappointment took material form, entered the phone line, traveled the distance between them, and crept into the inspector's ear in the form of an annoying itch.

"I need some information, signorina. What means of transport did Mr. Gargano normally use when he came to Vigàta?"

"He would come by car. His own."

"Let me rephrase that. Would he drive all the way from Bologna to here?"

"Certainly not. I always bought his return tickets. He would load the car onto the Palermo-Naples ferry, and I would reserve a single cabin for him."

He thanked her, hung up, and looked at Fazio.

"Here's what I want you to do."

7

As soon as he opened the door to his home, he realized Adelina had found a moment to come and tidy up. Everything was in order, the books dusted, the floor sparkling clean. But the housekeeper wasn't there. On the kitchen table he found a note:

Mr. Inspector, Im sending my neece Concetta to help out. She's a smart an hard workin girl an she gonna make you somtin to eat too. I come beck day afta tomorra.

Concetta had emptied the washer and spread everything out on the clothes rack. Montalbano's heart sank when he saw the sweater Livia had given him hanging there, reduced to the right size for a ten-year-old kid. It had shrunk. The girl hadn't realized that it was an article that should be washed at a different temperature from the rest. A feeling of panic came over him. He had to make it disappear, quick. Destroy all trace of it. The only hope was to burn it, reduce it to ashes. He grabbed it. No, it was still too damp. What to do? Yes, that was it: dig a deep pit in the sand and bury the corpus delicti. He could get to work straightaway, under cover of darkness, just like a murderer. He was about to open the French doors that gave out onto the veranda when the phone rang.

"Hello?"

"Hi, darling, how are you?"

It was Livia. Feeling absurdly as if he'd been caught in the act, he gave a little cry, dropping the accursed sweater to the floor and trying to hide it under the table with his foot.

"What's happening?" asked Livia.

"Nothing. I burned myself with my cigarette. Did you have a good holiday?"

"Fantastic. Just what I needed. And what about you? Any news?"

"The usual stuff."

For whatever reason, there was always an awkwardness between them, a kind of prudishness, whenever they tried to begin a conversation.

"As agreed, I'll be there day after to-morrow."

There? Where was "there"? Was Livia coming to Vigàta? Why? The idea pleased him, no doubt about that, but when had this been "agreed"? But there was no need to ask any questions; Livia knew by now what he was like.

"Naturally you've forgotten that we agreed on the date a couple of weeks ago. We said: better two days earlier."

"Come on, Livia, don't get upset, try to be patient."

"You would try the patience of a saint."

Oh, God, not another cliché! Sow your wild oats, count your chickens before they hatch, or eat like a horse, when you're not putting the cart first!

"Livia, I beg you, please don't talk that way."

"Sorry, darling, but I talk the way all normal people talk."

"So, am I abnormal, in your opinion?"

"Let's drop it, Salvo. We'd agreed I would come two days before Mimì's wedding. Or did you forget about Mimì's wedding too?"

"Actually, yes, I must confess I had forgotten about that, too. Fazio had to remind me that Mimì'd already gone on leave to get married. It's very strange."

"I don't find it strange at all," said Livia in a tone in which one could hear a polar ice pack forming.

"You don't? And why not?"

"Because you don't forget things, you repress them. It's completely different."

He realized he couldn't put up with this conversation much longer. Aside from clichés and stock phrases, he couldn't stand the sallies of cheap psychoanalysis that Livia all too often liked to indulge in — the kind of stuff you get in American movies where, say, some guy kills fifty-two people and then we find out that it's because one day, when he was a little kid, the serial killer's father wouldn't let him eat strawberry jam.

"What is it I'm repressing, in the learned opinion of you and your colleagues Freud and Jung?"

He heard a sardonic giggle at the other end.

"The very idea of marriage," Livia explained.

Polar bears were now wandering across the ice floes in her voice. What to do? React harshly and bring the conversation to a bad end? Or pretend submission, compliance, and equanimity? He opted tactically for the latter course.

"Maybe you're right," he said in a repentant tone.

It turned out to be a winning move, right on target.

"Let's drop the subject," Livia said magnanimously.

"Oh, no you don't! I think we should talk about it," Montalbano countered, realizing he was now on solid ground.

"Now? Over the phone? We'll talk about it calmly when I'm there."

"Okay. Don't forget we still have to buy a wedding present."

"You've got to be kidding!" Livia said, laughing.

"Don't you want to get him one?" asked Montalbano, confused.

"I've already bought the present and sent it off! Do you really think I would wait till the last day? I got a nice little thing I'm sure Mimì will like. I know his tastes."

There it was, right on schedule, the usual prick of jealousy. Utterly irrational, but always ready to answer the call.

"I'm sure you know Mimì's tastes quite well."

He couldn't help it; the thrust had come out by itself. A moment's pause from Livia, then the parry:

"Moron."

Another jab:

"And naturally you thought of Mimì's tastes and not Beatrice's."

"No, I checked with Beba by phone and asked her advice."

Montalbano no longer knew onto what ground he should move the skirmish. Lately their phone conversations had mainly become pretexts for squabbling. The best of it was that this animosity remained independent of the unshakable intensity of their relationship. But then why, when talking on the phone, did they quarrel, on average, at least once every four sentences? Maybe, thought the inspector, it was an effect of the distance between them becoming less and less tolerable with each passing day, since as we grow old — for every now and then one must, yes, look reality in the eye and call things by their proper names — we feel ever more keenly the need to have the person we love beside us. As he was reasoning along these lines (and he liked this line of reasoning, as it was reassuring and banal, like the sayings one finds on the little slip of paper inside Baci Perugina chocolates), he grabbed the sweater from under the table, put it in a plastic bag, opened the armoire, choked on the mothball stink, staggered backwards while kicking the armoire closed, then flung the bag on top of it. It could stay there for the time being. He would bury it before Livia arrived.

He opened the refrigerator and found nothing special there: a can of olives, another of anchovies, and a piece of *tumazzo* cheese. He cheered up, however, when he opened the oven. Concetta had prepared a platter of *patati cunsati,* an extremely simple dish that could be nothing or everything depending on the hand distributing the seasoning and orchestrating the interaction between the onions and capers, the olives and the vinegar and sugar, the salt and the pepper. At first bite, he became convinced that Concetta was a virtuoso in the kitchen and a worthy understudy to her auntie Adelina. After finishing the hefty platter of *patati cunsati,* he started eating bread and *tumazzo,* not because he was still hungry, but out of sheer gluttony. He remembered he'd always been a glutton and gourmand, ever since childhood. In fact his father used to call him *liccu cannarutu,* which meant just that, glutton and gourmand. The reminiscence was dragging him towards a twinge of emotion, but he boldly resisted with a splash of straight whisky. Then he got ready for bed. First, however, he wanted to find a book to

114

read. He couldn't decide between the latest book by Tabucchi and a novel by Simenon, an old one he had never read. As he was reaching out for the Tabucchi, the phone rang. To pick up or not to pick up, that was the question. The idiocy of the sentence that had popped into his mind so mortified him that he decided to answer, however great the hassle that might ensue.

"Am I disturbing you, Salvo? It's Mimì."

"Not at all."

"Were you about to go to bed?"

"Well, yes."

"Are you alone?"

"Who else would you expect to be here?"

"Could you give me five minutes?"

"Sure, go ahead."

"Not over the phone."

"Okay, come on over."

Mimì certainly didn't want to talk to him about work. About what, then? What could be the problem? Maybe he'd had a spat with Beatrice? A wicked thought entered the inspector's mind. If it turned out Mimì'd been quarreling with his fiancée, he would tell him to call Livia. After all, didn't he and Livia understand each other perfectly?

The doorbell rang. Who could that be, at

this hour? Mimì was out of the question, since it took at least ten minutes to drive from Vigàta to Marinella.

"Who is it?"

"It's me, Mimì."

How did he do that? Then Montalbano understood. Mimì must have been in the neighborhood and called him on his cell phone. He opened the door and his assistant came inside, looking pale, downcast, and long-suffering.

"Are you unwell?" Montalbano asked, concerned.

"Yes and no."

"What the hell does that mean, 'Yes and no'?"

"I'll explain in a minute. Could I have two shots of whisky, neat?" asked Mimì, sitting down in a chair next to the table.

The inspector, while pouring the whisky, suddenly froze. Hadn't they already acted out this exact same scene? Hadn't they said almost the exact same words?

Augello emptied his glass in a single gulp, stood up, went and poured himself another glass, and sat back down.

"Healthwise, I think I'm fine," he said. "That's not the problem."

For some time now, thought Montalbano, *whether in politics, economics, in the public or private spheres, "that" is never the problem.* Somebody will say: "There's too much unemployment," and the politician will answer: "Actually, that's not the problem." A husband will ask his wife: "Is it true you're cheating on me?" and she will answer: "That's not the problem." But since by now he remembered the script perfectly, he said to Mimì:

"You no longer want to get married."

Mimì looked at him, flabbergasted.

"Who told you?"

"Nobody. I can see it in your eyes, your face, your whole appearance."

"That's not exactly right. It's a complicated business."

Since "that" was not the problem, it was only natural that this would be "a complicated business." What would come next? That we were "getting ahead of ourselves" or that it was time to "move on"?

"The fact is," Mimì continued, "that I absolutely adore Beba. I like to make love to her, I like the way she thinks, the way she speaks, the way she dresses, the way she cooks —"

"But?" asked Montalbano, purposely interrupting him. Mimì had set out on a long and tortuous path: the list of the qualities of the woman one loves could be infinite,

117

like the names of the Lord.

"But I don't feel like marrying her."

Montalbano didn't breathe a word. Surely there was more to come.

"Or, rather, I do feel like marrying her, but . . ."

There was still more.

"Some nights I lie awake counting the hours left till I get married."

A tortured pause.

"On other nights I wish I could hop on the first flight out to Burkina Faso."

"Are there a lot of flights from here to Burkina Faso?" Montalbano asked with a cherubic expression.

Mimì abruptly stood up, red in the face.

"I'm leaving. I didn't come here to be made fun of."

Montalbano persuaded him to stay and talk. And Mimì embarked on a long monologue. The fact was, he explained, that one night he wanted one thing, the next night he wanted the opposite. He felt torn in two. One minute he felt afraid to take on obligations he couldn't meet, the next minute he was imagining himself a proud father of four. He couldn't make up his mind and was afraid he might cut and run at the moment of saying "I do," leaving everybody high and dry. And how could poor

Beba ever sustain such a blow?

Like the previous time, they polished off all the whisky there was in the house. The first to collapse was Mimì, already worn out from the previous nights and exhausted from his three-hour monologue. He got up and left the room. Montalbano thought he'd gone to the bathroom. He was wrong. Mimì had thrown himself diagonally across his bed and was snoring. The inspector cursed the saints, cursed Augello, lay down on the sofa, and little by little fell asleep.

He woke up with a headache, hearing somebody singing in the shower. Who could it be? Suddenly he remembered. He got up, aching all over from his uncomfortable sleep, and ran to the bathroom. Mimì was flooding the place as he showered. But he paid no mind and seemed happy. What to do? Knock him out with a blow to the base of the skull? Montalbano went out on the veranda. It was a passable day. He went back into the kitchen, made some coffee, poured himself a cup. Mimì made his entry, clean-shaven, fresh, and smiling.

"Is there any of that for me?"

Montalbano didn't answer. He didn't know what might come out of his mouth if he opened it. Mimì filled his cup halfway with sugar. The inspector felt like throwing up. The guy didn't drink coffee; he turned it into jam and ate it.

After drinking his coffee, or whatever it was, Mimì looked at him earnestly.

"Please forget everything I said to you last night. I've more than made up my mind to marry Beba. It was all bullshit, the kind of passing doubts that get into my head sometimes."

"May you bear only sons," Montalbano sullenly muttered. And as Augello was about to leave, he added, this time in a clear voice: "And my compliments, by the way."

Mimì turned around slowly, as if on his guard. The inspector's tone had been overtly insinuating.

"Your compliments for what?"

"For your work on the Gargano case. It's full of holes."

"Did you look at my files?" asked Augello, irritated.

"Don't worry, I prefer reading more informative things."

"Listen, Salvo," said Mimì, retracing his steps and sitting back down. "How do I have to explain to you that I only assisted in the investigation, and minimally at that? Everything's in Guarnotta's hands. Bologna's in on it too. So don't get upset with me. I only did what they told me to do. Period."

"Don't they have any idea where the money went?"

"They didn't for as long as I worked on the case. You know how these people operate: they move the money around from one country to another, one bank to another, setting up companies like Chinese boxes, offshore firms and that kind of stuff, so that you end up wondering if the money ever existed in the first place."

"So the only person who knows where the loot is would be Gargano?"

"In theory, he would be the only one."

"Explain."

"Well, I guess we can't exclude the possibility he might have had an accomplice. Or that he confided in someone. But I, for one, don't think he would have."

"Why not?"

"He wasn't the type. He didn't trust his coworkers, kept everything under tight control. The only person with even a little autonomy at the office — and I mean very little — was Giacomo Pellegrino. I think that was his name, or at least that's what the other two employees said, those two women. I wasn't able to question him because he's in Germany and hasn't come back yet."

"Who told you he went away?"

"His landlady did."

"Are you sure Gargano didn't disappear, or wasn't made to disappear, somewhere around here?"

"Look, Salvo, nobody's come up with any kind of train, boat, or airline ticket proving he went anywhere in the days before his disappearance. Maybe he came here by car, we told ourselves. He did have a digital highway pass, but there's no record of his having used it. Paradoxically, Gargano may never have budged from Bologna. Nobody's seen his car around here, and it'd be pretty hard to miss."

He looked at his watch.

"Is there anything else? I wouldn't want Beba to start worrying about me not being at home."

This time Montalbano, feeling in a better mood, stood up and accompanied him to the door. Not because Augello had made things seem any easier by what he'd said. But for the exact opposite reason. The difficulty of the case actually made him feel strangely happy and cheerful inside, rather the way the genuine hunter feels when faced with a shrewd, skilled prey.

In the doorway, Mimì asked him:

"Would you please tell me why you're getting so worked up over the Gargano case?"

"No. I probably don't even know myself. But while we're on the subject, any idea how François is doing?"

"I talked to my sister yesterday and she said they're all doing fine. You'll see them at the wedding. But why did you say 'while we're on the subject'? What has François got to do with Gargano?"

It would take too long and too much effort to explain the fright he'd had when it occurred to him the kid's money might have disappeared with the swindling *ragioniere*. That fright, in fact, had been one of the reasons he'd thrown himself headlong into the investigation.

"Is that what I said? Bah, I dunno," he replied with a perfect poker face.

"Fazio, forget what I said to you yesterday. Mimì told me they've been doing a lot of serious investigation. No sense in you wasting any more of your time. In any case, they can't even find a dog who's seen Gargano around here."

"Whatever you say, Chief," said Fazio.

But he didn't move from where he was standing in front of the inspector's desk.

"Did you want to tell me something?"

"I dunno. I found something in Inspector Augello's file. It's a deposition by someone who says he saw Gargano's Alfa 166 on a country road on the night of August the thirty-first."

Montalbano leapt out of his chair.

"Yeah, and?"

"Inspector Augello wrote next to it: 'Not to be taken seriously.' So they let it drop."

"Why, for the love of God?"

" 'Cause the man's name is Antonino Tommasino."

"What the fuck do I care what his name is! What matters is —"

"You should care, Chief. A couple of years ago this Tommasino went to the carabinieri and reported seeing a sea monster with three heads in the waters off Puntasecca. Then last year he came to our station at the crack of dawn screaming that he'd seen a flying saucer land. You shoulda seen it, Chief. He told his story to Catarella, who got so spooked he started screaming too. It was total pandemonium, Chief."

8

He'd been over an hour signing some papers Fazio had plopped down on his desk with an air of authority — "Chief, you absolutely have to take care of these, and you're not to move from here until you've finished!" — when the door opened and Augello came in without even knocking. He looked very upset.

"The wedding's been postponed!"

Oh God, his waffling must have taken a turn for the worse.

"You changed your mind like a good cuckold?"

"No, this morning Beba got a call from her hometown of Aidone. Her father's had a heart attack. Apparently it's not too serious, but she doesn't want to get married without her father. They're very close. She's already left and I'm going to join her later today. If all goes well, we'll have the wedding in about a month. What am I going to do?"

"What do you mean?" asked Montalbano, puzzled by the question.

"I can't hold out for a whole month, lying awake one night counting the days till the wedding, and the next night figuring out ways to run away. By the time I'm walking down the aisle I'll be either in a straitjacket or having a nervous breakdown."

"I'll keep you from having a nervous breakdown. Tell you what. You go to Aidone, see how things stand, then come back here and you can get back to work."

He reached for the telephone.

"I'm going to tell Livia."

"No need, I already called her," said Mimì, on his way out.

Montalbano felt a jealous rage well up inside. What? Your future father-in-law has a heart attack, your fiancée's crying and desperate, your wedding's down the drain, and the first thing you do is call Livia? He took a big swipe at the stack of papers, scattering them all over the floor, got up, left, drove to the port, and went on a long walk to dispel his fury.

He didn't know why, but on his way back to the station he decided to go a different way and passed in front of the King Midas office. It was open. He pushed on the glass door and went inside.

A sense of desolate bleakness immediately grabbed him by the throat. Only one lamp in the office was turned on, shedding a funereal light, as at a wake. Mariastella Cosentino sat behind her teller's window, immobile, eyes staring fixedly ahead.

"Good morning," said Montalbano. "I was just passing by and. . . . Any news?"

Mariastella threw up her hands and said nothing.

"Has Giacomo Pellegrino called in from Germany?"

Mariastella opened her eyes wide.

"From Germany?"

"Yes, he went to Germany on an assignment for Gargano. Didn't you know?"

Mariastella looked confused, disturbed.

"No, I didn't. In fact I was wondering what had become of him. I thought maybe he hadn't shown up to avoid —"

"No," said Montalbano. "His uncle, who's got the same name as him, told me Gargano had instructed Giacomo, by phone, to go to Germany on the afternoon of August the thirty-first."

"The day before Mr. Gargano was supposed to arrive?"

"Precisely."

Mariastella remained speechless.

"Something not seem right to you?"

"To be honest, yes."

"Tell me."

"Well, Giacomo was the only one of us who actually worked with Mr. Gargano on payments and calculation of interest. It seems odd to me that Mr. Gargano would send him so far away on business when he needed him more here. And anyway, Giacomo. . . ."

She stopped, clearly not wanting to go on.

"Go on, you can trust me. Tell me everything you're thinking. It's in Mr. Gargano's own interest."

Uttering the last sentence, he felt worse than a cheater at three-card monte. But Miss Cosentino swallowed the bait.

"I don't think Giacomo really knew much about high finance. Whereas Mr. Gargano did. He was a wizard."

Her eyes sparkled at the thought of her beloved's brilliance.

"Listen," said the inspector. "Do you know Giacomo Pellegrino's address?"

"Of course," said Mariastella.

She wrote it down for him.

"If you hear any news, give me a call," said Montalbano.

They shook hands, Mariastella limiting herself to exhaling a less than audible

"Good day." Perhaps she had no strength left. Perhaps she was letting herself starve to death the way some dogs do over the graves of their masters. He raced out of the office, feeling as if he were suffocating.

The door to Giacomo Pellegrino's apartment was wide open. There were sacks of cement, cans of paint, and other mason's equipment cluttering the landing. The inspector went inside.

"Can I come in?"

"What do you want?" a mason in mason's getup, paper hat and all, called out from atop a ladder.

"I dunno," said Montalbano, slightly disoriented. "Isn't this where somebody named Pellegrino lives?"

"I don't know nothing 'bout who lives or don't live here," said the mason.

He reached up and rapped his knuckles against the ceiling as if it were a door.

"Signora Catarina!" he called.

A woman's muffled voice answered from above.

"What is it?"

"Come downstairs, signora, there's someone here wants to talk to you."

"I'll be right down."

Montalbano stepped out onto the

landing. He heard a door open and close upstairs, then a strange noise that sounded like a bellows in action. It all became clear to him when he saw Signora Catarina appear at the top of the stairs. She must have weighed no less than three hundred pounds, and with every step she took, she made that huffing sound. As soon as she saw the inspector, she stopped.

"And who are you?"

"I'm a police inspector. Montalbano's the name."

"What do you want from me?"

"To talk to you, signora."

"Will it take long?"

The inspector made an evasive gesture with his hand. Signora Catarina looked at him thoughtfully.

"It's better if you come upstairs," she finally decided, beginning the difficult maneuver of turning herself around.

The inspector lingered. He would wait until he heard the key turn in the door upstairs before he moved.

"Come on up," the woman's voice guided him.

He found himself in the right living room. Madonnas under bell jars, reproductions of tearful Madonnas, little Madonna-shaped bottles full of Lourdes water. The signora was already seated in an armchair that had obviously been made to measure. She signaled to Montalbano to sit down on the sofa.

"Tell me something, Mr. Inspector. I was expecting this! I could sense he would end up this way, that degenerate hoodlum! In jail! Behind bars for his whole life, till the day he dies!"

"Who are you talking about, signora?"

"Who do you think? My husband! He's been out of the house for three days straight! Gambling, drinking, whoring, the vile, filthy wretch!"

"I'm sorry, signora, but I didn't come here because of your husband."

"Ah, no? So who'd you come for, then?"

"For Giacomo Pellegrino. He was renting the apartment downstairs, wasn't he?" The sort of globe that was Signora Catarina's face began to look more and more bloated, and the inspector was beginning to fear it might explode. In reality the woman was smiling with delight.

"Now there's a fine boy for you! So educated and polite! I'm so sorry I lost him!"

"You lost him in what sense?"

"I lost him because he left my house."

"He no longer lives downstairs?"

"No, sir."

"Please tell me the whole story from the beginning, signora."

"What beginning?" she said in dialect. "Roundabout the twenty-fifth of August, he comes up here and tells me he's gonna move out, and since he din't give no advance notice, he puts three months' rent in my hands. On the thirtieth, in the morning, he packed two suitcases with his stuff, said good-bye to me, and left the apartment empty. And that's the beginning and the end."

"Did he say where he was going to live?"

"An' why should he tell me that? What are we? Mother and son? Husband and wife? Brother and sister?"

"Not even cousins?" asked Montalbano, offering another variation on the possibilities of relation. But Signora Catarina didn't grasp the irony.

"Not a chance! All he said to me was he was going to Germany for about a month, but when he got back he was gonna move into his own house. Such a good boy. May the good Lord stand by him and help him!"

"Has he written or phoned you from Germany?"

"Why would he do that? What are we, relatives or something?"

"I think we've well established the answer to that question," said Montalbano. "Has anyone come looking for him?"

"No, sir, nobody. Except around the fourth or fifth of September, when somebody did come looking for him."

"Do you know who it was?"

"Yessir, a p'liceman. He said Mr. Giacomo was supposed to report to the p'lice station. But I told him he left for Germany."

"Did he have a car?"

"Who, Giacomino? No, he knew how to drive, had his license and all, but he din't have no car. He had a little broken-down motorbike. Sometimes it'd start, sometimes it wouldn't."

Montalbano stood up, thanked her, and said good-bye.

" 'Scuse me if I don't walk you to the door," said Signora Catarina, "but it's hard for me to stand up."

"Reason with me for a minute," said the inspector to the red mullets he had on his plate. "According to what Signora Catarina told me, Giacomo left the house on the morning of August the thirtieth. According to his namesake uncle, the next day Giacomo told him he was flying to

Germany at four o'clock that afternoon. So the question is this: Where did Giacomo sleep on the night of the thirtieth? Wouldn't it have been more logical to leave the apartment on the morning of the thirty-first after spending the night there? And also: What happened to the motorbike? But the main question is: Is Giacomo's story of any importance to the investigation? And, if so, why?" The mullets did not answer, among other reasons because they were no longer on the plate but in Montalbano's belly.

"Let's proceed as if it was important," he concluded.

"Fazio, I want you to check if there was a reservation for Giacomo Pellegrino on the four o'clock flight for Germany on August the thirty-first."

"For where in Germany?"

"I don't know."

"Chief, there are a lot of cities in Germany."

"You trying to be funny?"

"No, Chief. And out of which airport? Palermo or Catania?"

"Palermo, I would say. And now get outta here."

"Yes, sir. I just wanted to tell you that

Headmaster Burgio phoned to remind you of something you're supposed to know about."

Burgio, the retired secondary-school headmaster, had called the inspector some ten days earlier to invite him to a debate between those in favor and those against building a bridge over the Strait of Messina. Burgio was to be spokesman for those in favor. At the end of the meeting, who knows why, there was going to be a projection of Roberto Benigni's *Life Is Beautiful*. Montalbano had promised to attend to please his friend, but also to see the film, about which he'd heard contrasting opinions.

He decided to go to Marinella to change clothes, since the jeans he was wearing seemed a little out of place. He got in his car, drove home, and had the unfortunate idea to lie down on his bed for a moment, not more than five minutes. He slept for three hours straight. Waking up with a start, he realized that if he hurried, he could get there just in time for the movie.

The auditorium was jam-packed. The inspector arrived just as the lights were dimming. He remained standing. Every now and then he laughed. But things changed towards the end, and he began to feel a sadness welling up in his throat . . . Never before had he cried while watching a film. He left the auditorium before the lights came back on, embarrassed that someone might see that his eyes were wet with tears. So why had it happened to him this time? Because of his age? Was it a sign of aging? It's true that as one gets older one becomes more easily moved. But that wasn't the only reason. Was it because of the story the film told and the way it told it? Of course, but that didn't explain it, either. He waited outside for the people to exit so he could say hello to Burgio in passing. He felt like being alone and went straight home.

The wind was blowing on the veranda, and it was cold. The sea had eaten up almost the whole beach. He kept a raincoat in the front closet, the kind with a lining. He put it on, went back out on the veranda, and sat down. He was unable, in the gusts, to light a cigarette. He would have to go back in his bedroom to do so. Rather than get up, he decided not to smoke. Out on the water he saw some distant lights that every few moments would disappear. If they were fishermen, they were having a rough time of it, on that sea. He sat there motionless, hands thrust in the pockets of his raincoat, rehashing what had come over him while watching the film. All at once, the true and sole reason for his weeping became perfectly clear to him. And just as quickly, he rejected it as unbelievable. Yet little by little, in spite of the fact that he kept circling around it, to attack it from every angle, that reason stood firm. In the end, he had to give in to it. And so he made up his mind.

Before setting out the next morning, he had to wait at the Bar Albanese for the fresh ricotta cannoli to arrive. He bought about thirty of them, along with a few kilos of *biscotti regina,* marzipan pastries, and *mostaccioli.* Rolling along, his car left an aromatic cloud in its wake. He had no choice but to keep the windows open, otherwise the intense smell would have given him a headache.

To get to Calapiano he chose to take the longest, roughest road, the one he'd always taken the few times he'd gone there, since it allowed him a glimpse of a Sicily that was disappearing a little more each day, made up of land spare in vegetation and men spare in words. After he'd been driving for two hours, just past Gagliano he found himself at the back of a line of cars moving very slowly along the beat-up macadam. A handwritten sign on a lamp-post ordered:

SLOW DOWN!

Then a man with the face of an escaped convict (but are we so sure escaped convicts have faces like that?), in civilian dress and with a whistle in his mouth, blew his whistle hard like a referee and raised his arm. The car in front of Montalbano immediately stopped. After a minute or two in which nothing happened, the inspector decided to stretch his legs. He got out of the car and went up to the man.

"Are you a policeman?"

"Me? Not on your life! Gaspare Indelicato's the name. I'm a maintenance man at the elementary school. Please step aside, there are cars coming this way."

"Excuse me, but isn't today a school day?"

"Of course, but the school is closed. Two ceilings collapsed."

"Is that why you were assigned traffic duty?"

"Nobody assigned me anything. I volunteered. If I wasn't here and Peppi Brucculeri — who also volunteered —

wasn't over there, can you imagine the mess?"

"What happened to the road?"

"It caved in about a kilometer from here. Five months ago. There's only room for one car to pass at a time."

"Five months ago?!"

"Yessirree. The town council says it's the provincial council that should repair it, the provincial council says it's the job of the regional council, the regional council says it's up to the road department, and you, in the meantime, get screwed."

"And you don't?"

"I get around on bicycle."

Half an hour later, Montalbano was able to resume his journey. He remembered that the farm was about four kilometers outside of Calapiano, and to get there one had to take a little dirt road so full of holes, rocks, and dust that even goats shunned it. This time, however, he found himself on a road that was narrow, yes, but paved and well maintained. There were two possibilities: He had either made a wrong turn or the town of Calapiano had an efficient administration. The latter proved to be the case. The big farmhouse appeared round a bend, a light plume of smoke rising from the chimney, a sign that somebody was cooking in the kitchen. He looked at his watch. It was almost one o'clock. He got out of the car, filled his arms with cannoli and pastries, went into the house and into the big room that served as both dining and living room, as demonstrated by the television in the corner. He put his packages down on the table and went into the kitchen. Franca, Mimì's sister, had her back to him and didn't realize he'd come in. The inspector stood there a moment, watching her in silence, admiring the harmony of her movements but mostly spellbound by the aroma of ragù filling his lungs.

"Franca."

The woman turned around, face lighting up, and ran into Montalbano's arms.

"Salvo! What a big surprise!" she said. Then: "Have you heard about Mimì's wedding?"

"Yes."

"Beba phoned me this morning; her father's feeling better."

She said no more and went back to the stove. She didn't bother to ask Salvo why he'd come to see them.

What a woman! thought Montalbano. Then he asked:

"Where are the others?"

"The grown-ups are working. Giuseppe, Domenico, and François are at school. But they'll be back soon. Ernst has gone in the car to pick them up. Remember him? The German student who spent the summer here lending a hand? He liked it so much, he comes back whenever he can."

"I need to talk to you," said Montalbano.

He told her about the passbook and the money he'd entrusted to the notary. He'd never mentioned it before to either Franca or her husband, Aldo, for the simple reason that he always forgot. As he was explaining, Franca kept going back and forth between the kitchen and the dining room, the inspector following behind her. When he'd finished, her only comment was:

"You did the right thing. I'm so happy for François. Want to help me set the table?"

9

When he heard the car pull into the courtyard, he couldn't help himself and ran outside.

He recognized François at once. God, how he'd changed! He was no longer the little boy he remembered, but a lanky youth with dark, curly hair and big dark eyes. At that same moment François saw him.

"Salvo!"

And he flew to him and hugged him tight. Not like the time when he'd run towards him and then sidestepped at the last second. Now there were no more problems between them, no more shadows, only great affection, and Salvo could feel it in the intensity and duration of their embrace. And thus, with Montalbano resting a hand on François's shoulder and the boy trying to wrap his arm around the inspector's waist, they went into the house, followed by the others.

Then Aldo and his three helpers arrived and they all sat down at the table. François was sitting at Montalbano's right, and at a certain point the boy's hand came to rest on Salvo's knee. The inspector moved his fork out of his right hand and contrived somehow to eat his pasta al ragù with his left, keeping his other hand on top of the boy's. Whenever the two hands had to quit each other's company to take a sip of wine or to cut a piece of meat, they would come immediately back for their secret rendez-vous under the table.

"If you want to rest, there's a room ready," said Franca when they had finished eating.

"No, I'm going to leave right away."

Aldo and his helpers stood up, said good-bye to Montalbano, and went out.

Giuseppe and Domenico did the same.

"They're going to work until five," Franca explained. "Then they'll come back and do their homework."

"And what about you?" Montalbano asked François.

"I'm staying here with you until you leave. I want to show you something."

"Go," Franca said to both of them. Then, turning to Montalbano: "In the meantime I'll write down what you asked me."

François led him round behind the

house, where there was a big meadow of alfalfa. Four horses were grazing in it.

"Bimba!" François called.

A young mare with a blond mane raised her head and came towards the boy. When she was within reach, François started running and with a leap he was on the animal's bare back. He made a circle and returned.

"Do you like her?" François asked happily. "Papa gave her to me."

Papa? He must mean Aldo, of course. He was right to call him papa. Still, for a brief moment it was a pinprick to the heart. Nothing, really, but he felt it.

"I also showed Livia what a good rider I am," said François.

"Oh, you did?"

"Yes, the other day, when she came to visit. She was afraid I would fall off. You know how women are."

"Did she sleep here?"

"Yeah, one night. Then she left the next day. Ernst drove her back to the airport. I was so happy to see her."

Montalbano said nothing, didn't even breathe. They walked back towards the house in silence, just like before, with the inspector's arm around the boy's shoulders and François trying to embrace him

144

around the waist but actually clutching his jacket. At the door François said in a low voice:

"I want to tell you a secret."

Montalbano bent down.

"When I grow up, I want to be a policeman like you."

For the drive back he took the other road, and instead of taking four and a half hours it took only three. At the station he was immediately assailed by Catarella, who seemed more distressed than usual.

"Ah, Chief, Chief! Hizzoner mister c'mishner says that —"

"Out of my hair, both of you."

Catarella was crushed. He didn't even have the strength to react.

Once inside his office, Montalbano set about frantically searching for a sheet of paper and envelope without the Vigàta Police letterhead. He succeeded. Then he sat down and wrote a letter to the commissioner with no formal greeting whatsoever.

I hope by now you've received the copy of the notary's letter I anonymously sent to you. Included herewith you'll find all the documents pertaining to the lawful adoption of the child you

145

actually accused me of having kid-napped. I, for my part, consider the matter settled. If you persist in pur-suing it, let me warn you that I will sue you for slander.

Montalbano

"Catarella!"

"Yessir, Chief!"

"Here's a thousand lire. Go buy a stamp, stick it on this envelope, and mail it."

"But, Chief, there's stamps galore in this office!"

"Do as I say. Fazio!"

"Yessir."

"Any news?"

"Yes, Chief. And I have to thank a friend of mine with the airport police who's got a friend whose girlfriend works at the ticket counter at Punta Raisi. That was a lucky break. Otherwise we would've waited at least three months for an answer."

The Italian method for streamlining bureaucracy. Fortunately there's always somebody who knows somebody who knows somebody else.

"And so?"

Fazio, who wanted to relish his hard-earned triumph, took an eternity to slip his hand in his pocket, pull out a folded sheet of paper, unfold it, and hold it in front of him as a guide.

"It turns out that Giacomo Pellegrino had a ticket, issued by the Icarus Travel Agency of Vigàta, for a four p.m. flight on August the thirty-first. And you know what? He never got on that flight."

"Is that certain?"

"Gospel, Chief. But you don't seem too surprised."

"I was feeling more and more convinced that Pellegrino never left."

"Let's see if you're surprised by what I tell you next. Pellegrino showed up in person, two hours before departure, to cancel his flight."

"At two o'clock, in other words."

"Right. Then he changed destination."

"Now I'm surprised," Montalbano conceded. "Where'd he go?"

"Wait. It doesn't end there. He booked a flight for Madrid, first of September, ten a.m., but . . ."

Fazio grinned triumphantly. Perhaps in the background he was hearing the march from *Aïda*. He opened his mouth to speak, but the inspector knavishly beat him to the punch line.

". . . but he didn't get on that one, either," he concluded.

Fazio, visibly irritated, crumpled the sheet and shoved it unceremoniously back in his pocket.

"It's no use with you. You're no fun at all."

"Come on, don't get upset," the inspector consoled him. "How many travel agencies are there in Montelusa?"

"There are three more right here in Vigàta."

"I'm not interested in the ones in Vigàta."

"I'll go look it up in the phone book and get you the numbers."

"Don't bother. Call them yourself and ask if, at any time between the twenty-eighth of August and the first of September, there were any reservations made in the name of Giacomo Pellegrino."

Fazio looked dumbfounded. Then he shook himself out of it.

"It can't be done. Working hours are over. I'll take care of it tomorrow morning as soon as I come in. But, Chief, if I find out this Pellegrino made still another reservation for, I dunno, Moscow or London, what does it mean?"

"It means our friend wanted to muddy the waters. He's got his ticket to Madrid in his pocket, when in fact he told everyone he was going to Germany. Tomorrow we'll find out if he had any other tickets in his pocket. Have you got Mariastella Cosentino's home phone number anywhere?"

"I'll go check Augello's files."

He went out, came back with a scrap of paper, dictated the number to Montalbano, and left. The inspector dialed the number. There was no answer. Maybe Miss Cosentino had gone out grocery shopping. He put the scrap of paper in his pocket and decided to go home to Marinella.

He had no appetite. The pasta al ragù and pork he'd eaten at Franca's sat a little heavy on his stomach. He fried himself an egg, then ate four fresh anchovies tossed in oil, vinegar, and oregano. After eating, he tried Miss Cosentino's number again. She must have been waiting with her hand over the phone, because she answered before the first ring had time to finish. The voice of a dying woman, thin as a spiderweb, said:

"Hello? Who's this?"

"Montalbano here. Sorry to bother you, perhaps you were watching television and —"

"I don't have a television."

The inspector didn't know why, but he

had the impression he'd heard a distant, faraway bell ring very briefly in his brain. It was so quick, so sudden, that he wasn't really sure if he'd heard right or not.

"I wanted to know, if you still remember, of course, whether Giacomo Pellegrino didn't come to work on the thirty-first of August, either."

Her response came immediately, without the slightest hesitation.

"Inspector, I could never forget those days, since I've gone over them time and again in my mind. On the thirty-first, Pellegrino showed up late for work, around eleven. And he left almost immediately; he said he had to meet with a client. He came back after lunch, probably around four-thirty, and stayed until closing time."

The inspector thanked her and hung up.

It made sense, added up. Pellegrino, after going to talk to his uncle in the morning, comes in to work. At midday he goes out, not to meet with a client, but to catch a cab or pick up a rental car. He goes to Punta Raisi, arriving at the airport around two, cancels the ticket for Berlin and books a flight to Madrid instead. He gets back in the cab or the rental car, and by four-thirty he's back at the office. The timing worked out.

But why did Pellegrino go to all this trouble? Granted, so he couldn't be easily tracked down. But by whom? And, most of all, why? Whereas the *ragioniere* Gargano had twenty billion reasons for vanishing, Pellegrino, to all appearances, had none.

"Hi, darling. Did you have a rough day today?"

"Livia, could you wait just a second?"

"Sure."

He pulled up a chair, sat down, fired up a cigarette, and got comfortable. He was sure this would be a very long phone call.

"I'm a little tired, but it's not from working too hard."

"So what is it, then?"

"All told, I did almost eight hours of driving today."

"Where'd you go?"

"To Calapiano, darling."

Livia must have suddenly found herself short of breath, because the inspector clearly heard a kind of sob. He generously waited for her to get hold of herself, then let her do the talking.

"Did you go because of François?"

"Yes."

"Is he sick?"

"No."

"So why did you go?"

"Aviva spinno."

"Don't start talking in dialect, Salvo! You know there are times when I just can't stand it! What did you say?"

"I said I felt like seeing him. *Spinno* means 'wish' or 'desire.' Now that you understand the word, let me ask you. Have you never felt the *spinno* to go see François?"

"You're such a swine, Salvo."

"Shall we make a deal? I won't speak dialect if you won't insult me. Okay?"

"Who told you I'd been to see François?"

"He did himself, when he was showing me what a good horseman he is. The grown-ups played along with you. They respected your agreement and didn't say a word. Because it's obvious you begged them not to tell me you'd been there. Whereas to me you said you had a day off and were going to the beach with a friend, and I, like an idiot, swallowed the bait. But tell me something, I'm curious: Did you tell Mimì you were going to Calapiano?"

He was expecting a violent response, a tiff for the ages. But Livia burst into tears, and long, painful, desperate sobs.

"Livia, listen . . ."

The call was cut off.

He stood up calmly, went into the bathroom, undressed, washed, and, before leaving the room, looked at himself in the mirror. For a long time. Then he gathered together all the saliva he had in his mouth and spit at his reflection in the mirror. Then he turned off the lights and went to bed. He got up at once because the telephone was ringing. He picked up the receiver, but the person at the other end said nothing. All he could hear was breathing. Montalbano recognized that breathing.

He began to speak, and he monologued for nearly an hour, with no crying, no tears, though his words were as sorrowful as Livia's sobs. And he told her things he'd never wanted to admit to himself, how he wounded others so as not to be wounded, how for some time now he'd discovered that his solitude was no longer a strength but a weakness, and what a bitter experience it had been for him to realize the very simple and natural fact that he was aging. In the end, Livia said simply:

"I love you."

Before hanging up, she added:

"I haven't canceled my vacation time yet. I'll stay here another day and then come to Vigàta. Free yourself of all commitments; I want you all to myself."

Montalbano went back to bed. He barely had time to crawl under the covers before he closed his eyes and fell asleep. He entered the country of sleep with the light step of a little kid.

It was eleven o'clock when Fazio came into Montalbano's office.

"Chief, you want to hear the latest? Pellegrino bought a ticket for Lisbon at the Intertour Travel Agency of Montelusa. The flight left at three-thirty in the afternoon on the thirty-first. I called Punta Raisi, and it turns out Pellegrino got on that plane."

"Do you believe it?"

"Why shouldn't I?"

"Because he probably sold his seat to somebody on the waiting list. But mostly because he came back to the office here, in Vigàta. That much is certain. At five o'clock he was at the King Midas agency. Therefore he couldn't have been on a flight for Lisbon."

"So what does it mean?"

"It means that Pellegrino is a fool who thinks he's clever but is only a fool. Do something for me. Ask around at all the hotels, guesthouses, and bed-and-breakfasts in Vigàta and Montelusa whether

Pellegrino spent the night of the thirtieth at one of their establishments."

"Right away."

"One more thing: Inquire at all the car rental agencies whether Pellegrino rented any cars around the same time."

"But why were we looking for Gargano before, and now we're looking for Pellegrino?" asked Fazio, looking doubtful.

"Because I've become convinced that as soon as we find one we'll know exactly where to find the other. You want to bet on it?"

"No, sir. I would never bet against you," said Fazio, going out.

Yet had he accepted the bet, he would have won.

The inspector felt his customary wolflike hunger come over him, perhaps because he'd slept better than he had in a long time. Unburdening himself to Livia had made him feel lighter and brought him back within himself. He felt like joking around. When Calogero came to recite the brief litany of the menu, he interrupted him at once.

"Today I feel like Wiener schnitzel," he said.

"Really?" said Calogero, dumbfounded

and leaning on the table to keep from falling over.

"And do you really think I'd ask *you* for a Wiener schnitzel? It'd be like asking a Buddhist monk to recite the Mass. What've you got today?"

"Spaghetti in squid ink."

"Bring me some. And for the second course?"

"Baby octopus dumplings."

"Bring me a dozen of those, too."

At six o'clock that evening, Fazio reported back to him.

"Chief, it looks like he didn't sleep anywhere that night. He did, on the other hand, rent a car in Montelusa on the morning of the thirty-first. He returned it that same afternoon, at four. The receptionist there, who's a smart girl, told me the mileage would correspond to a trip to Palermo and back."

"It fits," the inspector commented.

"Oh, and the girl also said Pellegrino specified he wanted a car with a spacious trunk."

"I'm sure he did. He needed room for the two suitcases."

They both sat in silence for a moment.

"But where did the damned guy sleep?"

Fazio wondered aloud.

The effect his words had on the inspector gave him a scare. Indeed, Montalbano looked at him goggle-eyed and then slapped himself hard on the forehead.

"What an idiot!"

"What'd you say?" asked Fazio, ready to apologize.

Montalbano stood up, took something from a drawer, and put it in his pocket.

"Let's go."

10

In the car, Montalbano began racing in the direction of Montelusa as if he were being tailed. When he turned onto the road that led to Pellegrino's recently constructed villa, Fazio's face turned to stone; he stared straight ahead and didn't open his mouth. Pulling up in front of the locked gate, the inspector stopped and they got out. The broken windowpanes had not been replaced, but someone had affixed plastic wrap over them with pushpins. The word "ASSHOLE" in green on the four walls had not been removed.

"There might be somebody inside, maybe the uncle," said Fazio.

"Let's play it safe," said the inspector. "Call the station and get the phone number of Giacomo Pellegrino, the one who filed the report. Then call him and tell him you came here to make an inspection, and ask him if it was him that put the plastic over the windows. Also ask him if he has any news of his nephew. If there's no answer, we'll decide what to do."

As Fazio was making his phone calls, Montalbano headed towards the felled olive tree. It had since lost the better part of its leaves, which now lay scattered and yellow on the ground. Clearly it wouldn't be long before it changed from a living tree to inert wood. The inspector then did something strange, or, rather, childlike: He went up to a spot around the middle of the tree and put his ear against it, as one might do to a dying man to listen if his heart is still beating. He stayed there a few minutes. What was he doing, trying see if he could hear the flow of the sap? He started laughing. This was the stuff of Baron von Münchausen, where one needed only put one's ear to the ground to hear the grass grow. He hadn't noticed that Fazio, from afar, had witnessed his whole routine and was now approaching.

"Chief, I talked with the uncle. It was him that covered the windows, because his nephew had left him the key to the front gate, but not to the house. And he has no news of him from Germany, but he says he should be back soon." Then he looked at the olive tree and shook his head.

"Look at this massacre!" said Montalbano.

"Asshole," said Fazio, intentionally using

the same word the inspector had written on the walls.

"Now do you understand why I had such a fit?"

"You don't owe me any explanation," said Fazio. "So what do we do now?"

"Now we go inside," said Montalbano, pulling out the little sack he'd taken from a drawer in his desk, which contained a rich assortment of picklocks and skeleton keys given him by a burglar friend. "You watch out and make sure no one's coming."

He fiddled with the lock on the gate and opened it fairly easily. The front door to the house was more difficult, but in the end he succeeded. He called Fazio.

They went inside. A big, entirely empty living room spread out before them. Also devoid of the slightest object were the kitchen and bathroom. In the living room a staircase of stone and wood led upstairs. Here there were two spacious bedrooms, unfurnished. In the second of these, however, laid out on the floor, was a kind of thick, brand-new blanket, barely used, with the company label still attached. The shelf under the bathroom mirror contained a variety of aerosol shaving cans and five disposable razors. Two had been used.

"Giacomo did the most logical thing

there was to do. When he left his rental apartment, he came here. He slept on this blanket. But where are the two suitcases he brought with him?" said Montalbano.

They looked in the attic, and in a closet under the staircase. Nothing. They closed the door to this and then, just to be sure, circled round the outside of the house. In the back there was a little iron door, the upper half of which consisted of an open grid to allow air to circulate. Montalbano opened it. There was a kind of crawl space for tools. In the middle of it were two big suitcases.

They dragged them out, as the space was too small. The suitcases weren't locked. Montalbano took one, Fazio the other. They didn't know what they were looking for, but they looked anyway. Socks, underpants, shirts, handkerchiefs, a suit, a raincoat. They looked at each other, then shoved everything roughly back into the suitcases without exchanging a word. Fazio couldn't get his shut.

"Just leave it like that," the inspector ordered.

They put them back inside the crawl space, relocked the door and then the front gate, and left.

"Chief, none of this makes any sense to

me," said Fazio as they were approaching Vigàta. "If this Giacomo Pellegrino went on a long trip to Germany, why didn't he bring along even a single change of underwear? It seems unlikely he bought all new things."

"And there's another thing that doesn't make sense," said Montalbano. "Does it seem logical to you that we didn't find a single sheet or scrap of paper, a single letter or notebook or agenda?"

Once in Vigàta, the inspector turned down a narrow street that led away from the station.

"Where are we going?"

"I'm going to see Giacomo's former landlady. I want you to drive my car back to the station. I can walk there when I'm done, it's not very far."

"What's the problem?" asked Signora Catarina from behind the door, sounding like an asthmatic whale.

"It's Montalbano."

The door opened. A monstrous head appeared, bristling with plastic curlers shaped like little cannoli.

"I can't ask you in 'cause I'm in my negligee."

"I beg your pardon for the disturbance,

Signora Catarina. Just one question: How many suitcases did Giacomo Pellegrino have?"

"Didn't I already tell you? Two."

"And nothing else?"

"He also had a briefcase, a small one. He kept his papers in it."

"Do you know what kind of papers?"

"Do I look to you like the kind of person who goes sticking her nose into other people's things? What do you think I am, some kind of no-good busybody?"

"Signora Catarina, how could you think I could ever think such a thing? I merely meant that if the briefcase happened to be left open, somebody might get a glimpse of what's inside, by chance, you know, by accident . . ."

"Actually that did happen, once. But by accident, mind you. And there were all kinds of letters inside, and sheets of paper full of numbers, some agendas, and a few of those black things that look like little disks —"

"Computer diskettes?"

"Yeah, things like that."

"Did Giacomo have a computer?"

"He did. And he always carried it around with him, in a special case."

"Did he have an Internet connection?"

"Inspector, I don't know anything about these things. But I do remember one time when I had to talk to him about a leaky pipe, I tried phoning him and the line was always busy."

"Excuse me, signora, but why did you call him instead of just going downstairs?"

"You think it's nothing, going down a flight of stairs, but for me, with my weight —"

"I'm sorry, I wasn't thinking."

"Well, I called and called, but the line was always busy. So I gathered up my strength, went downstairs, and knocked on his door. I told Jacuminu he maybe left his phone off the hook. But he told me the line was busy 'cause he was connected to this Interneck."

"I see. So when he left he also took the briefcase and the computer?"

"Of course. What was he gonna do, leave 'em with me?"

Montalbano headed back to the station in a bad mood. It was true that he should have been pleased to learn that Pellegrino's papers did exist and that he'd probably taken them with him; but the fear of having to deal again with computers, diskettes, CD-ROMs and other such bothers — as he'd had to do in the case that came to be called the "Excursion to Tindari" —

made his stomach churn. Good thing there was Catarella to lend him a hand.

He recounted to Fazio what Signora Catarina had told him in both his first and second meetings with her.

"Okay," said Fazio, after thinking things over a little. "Let's assume Pellegrino escaped to a foreign country. The first question is: Why? He was not involved, in any direct way, in Gargano's scam. Only some nutcase like the late Mr. Garzullo could have ever held it against him. The second question is: Where did he get the money to build the new house?"

"There is one conclusion that can be drawn from this business of the house," said Montalbano.

"And what's that?"

"That Pellegrino wanted to go into hiding for a little while, but that he did want to come back sooner or later, preferably on the sly, and enjoy his little villa in peace. Otherwise why would he have built it? Unless some new and unforeseen development came up, forcing him to flee, maybe forever, and leave the house to the dogs."

"And there's another thing," Fazio resumed. "It's logical that he would take his documents, papers, and computer when leaving the country. But I really don't think he would bring his motorbike to Germany, if he ever went there."

"Call the uncle, see if he left it with him."

Fazio went out and came back a few minutes later.

"No, he didn't leave it with him. He doesn't know anything about it. Look, Chief, that uncle is starting to prick up his ears. He asked me why we're getting so interested in his nephew. He seemed worried. He'd always bought that story about the business trip to Germany."

"And now we're left high and dry," the inspector concluded.

A silence of defeat fell over them.

"But there's still something we can do," the inspector decided after a moment. "You, tomorrow morning, go and make the rounds of the banks in Vigàta and try to find out which one of them Pellegrino's got his money in. It's certainly not going to be in the same one as Gargano. If you've got any friends in the business, see if you can find out how much he's got, whether he's been depositing money on top of his salary, that kind of thing. And one last favor: What was the name of that guy who sees flying saucers and three-headed dragons?"

Before answering, Fazio made a puzzled face.

"Antonino Tommasino's his name. But I'm warning you, Chief: the guy's a raving lunatic, you can't take what he says seriously."

"Fazio, what does a man do when he's deathly ill and the doctors throw their hands up? To escape death, he's liable to turn to a wizard, a warlock, a charlatan. And we, my dear friend, at this hour of the night, we are on death's doorstep as far as this investigation is concerned. Give me the phone number."

Fazio went out and returned with a sheet of paper.

"This is his voluntary deposition. He says he has no phone."

"Does he have a home, at least?"

"Yes he does, Chief. But it's hard to get to. Want me to make you a map?"

As he was opening the door to his house, he noticed there was an envelope in the mailbox. Picking it up, he recognized Livia's handwriting. But there was no letter inside, only a newspaper clipping, an interview with an elderly philosopher who lived in Turin. Overcome with curiosity, he decided to read it at once, even before finding out what Adelina's niece had left him in the fridge. Talking about his family, the philosopher said at one point: "When you get old, affections count more than concepts."

He immediately lost his appetite. If, for a philosopher, there comes a moment when speculation means less than affection, then how much could a criminal investigation mean for a cop heading into the sunset? In spite of himself, he had to admit that there was only one answer to this question: that an investigation probably meant even less than a concept. He slept badly.

By six the next morning he was already out of the house. The day looked promising: bright, clear sky, no wind. He'd put the little map drawn by Fazio down on the passenger's seat beside him and consulted it from time to time. Tommasino Antonino or Antonino Tommasino, whatever the hell his name was, lived in the countryside near Montereale, and therefore was not too far from Vigàta. The problem lay in choosing the right route, for it was easy to get lost there. The landscape was a kind of treeless desert scarred with dirt roads, goat trails, and crawler tracks, and dotted here and there by peasant cottages and a few rare country houses. The area was doing its best to avoid being transformed overnight into a jumble of weekend getaway bungalows, but one could already see the first signs of the futility of such resistance: trenches for water mains, lampposts, telephone poles, foundations for out-and-out four-lane roads. He drove around inside the desert three or four times, always coming back to the same point. Fazio's map was too vague. Feeling lost, he headed resolutely towards a kind of farmstead. He pulled up and got out of the car. The door to the house was open.

"Anybody here?"

"Come in," a woman's voice called out.

He found himself in a tidy, well-kept sort of living-dining room with old but shiny furniture. A woman of about sixty, well groomed and dressed in gray, was drinking a cup of coffee, the espresso pot on the table still steaming.

"I just need some information, ma'am. I'd like to know where Mr. Antonino Tommasino lives."

"He lives right here. I'm his wife."

For some reason he'd imagined Tommasino as a semivagrant or, at best, a *viddrano,* a peasant farmer, that is, an endangered species in need of protection.

"I'm Inspector Montalbano."

"I recognized you," said the woman, nodding towards the television in the corner. "I'll go get my husband. In the meantime please have some coffee. I make it strong."

"Thank you."

She poured it for him, left the room, then reappeared almost at once.

"My husband asked if you could go to him, if it's not too much trouble."

They walked down a whitewashed corridor, and the woman gestured to him to go in the second door on the left. It was a genuine study, with tall shelves lined with books and old nautical maps on the walls. The man who got up from an armchair to greet him was also about sixty, tall and erect, with beautiful white hair and wearing an elegant blazer and eyeglasses. A fairly imposing figure. Montalbano had been convinced he would be up against a wild-eyed crackpot with a string of spittle hanging from a corner of his mouth. He felt confused. Was he certain there was no mistake?

"Are you Antonino Tommasino?" he asked. But he would have liked to add, just to be sure: the raving madman who sees monsters and flying saucers?

"Yes. And you are Inspector Montalbano. Please make yourself comfortable."

He sat him down in a cozy armchair.

"I'm at your service. What can I do for you?"

That indeed was the question. How to open the discussion without offending Mr. Tommasino, who seemed to be perfectly normal in the head, as far as that was concerned.

"Reading anything interesting these days?"

The question had slipped out, and it was so idiotic and absurd that the inspector blushed. Tommasino, for his part, smiled.

"I'm reading the so-called *Book of Roger*, by Al-Idrisi, the medieval Arab geographer. But you didn't come here to ask me what I'm reading. You came to find out what I saw one night a little over a month ago. I guess they've changed their minds down at the station."

"Yes, thank you," said Montalbano, grateful that the other had taken the initiative. He was not only normal, this Tommasino, but a refined, cultured, intelligent man.

"Just one thing, before we begin. What

171

did they tell you about me?"

Montalbano balked, embarrassed. Then he decided that it was always best to tell the truth.

"They said that, every now and then, you see things that don't exist."

"You're very kind, Inspector. To get right to the point, they say I'm a madman. A peaceable madman, of course, who pays his taxes, respects the law, never does anything obscene or violent, never threatens anyone or mistreats his wife, but a madman nonetheless. You put it perfectly: every now and then, I see things that don't exist."

"Excuse me," Montalbano interrupted him, "but what do you do?"

"You mean professionally? I used to teach geography at the secondary school in Montelusa. But I've been retired a few years. May I tell you a story?"

"Of course."

"I have a grandson, Michele, who's now fourteen. One day, about ten years ago, my son came to visit with his wife and son. Which he still does, I'm happy to say. Michele and I went to play outside. At a certain point, Michele started screaming, saying the courtyard was full of terrible, ferocious dragons. And I played along, and started howling in fear myself. But then the little boy got scared by my fear and wanted to reassure me. 'Grampa,' he said, 'those aren't real dragons. You're not supposed to be afraid. I just made them up, for fun.' You know, Inspector, for a few years now, I've been in a situation much like that of my young nephew. One part of my brain must, in some way, and for some mysterious reason, have regressed to the childhood level. With the difference that, unlike the child, I take what I see to be real and continue to believe it for some time. Then I get over it, and I realize that what I saw wasn't real. Is that clear so far?"

"Perfectly clear," said the inspector.

"May I ask you what they told you I saw?"

"Well, I think it was a three-headed sea monster and a flying saucer."

"Is that all? They didn't tell you about the flock of winged fish made of tin I saw perched in a tree? Or the time a midget from Venus popped up in my kitchen and asked me for a cigarette? Shall we stop here, before we stray too far off the track?"

"As you wish."

"Now, let's review the things I just mentioned and the things you already knew. A three-headed sea monster, a flying saucer, a flock of tin-winged fish, and a Venusian midget. Do you agree with me that none of these things are real?"

"Of course."

"Now, if I come to you and say, Look, the other night I saw a car that was like this or like that, why shouldn't you believe me? Do cars not exist? Are they objects of fantasy? I'm talking about an everyday thing, a real car, with four wheels, a license plate, registration. I'm not talking about a space scooter that can fly up to Mars!"

"Take me to the place where you saw Gargano's car," said Montalbano.

He'd found a precious witness. He was sure of it.

11

That brief moment spent inside the house had been enough for the weather to change. A bitter, cold wind had risen, with gusts like tremendous swipes of the paw of some ferocious beast. Fat, pregnant clouds were rolling in from the sea. Following Mr. Tommasino's directions as he drove, Montalbano tried, in the meantime, to get him to explain things better.

"Are you sure it was the night of August the thirty-first?"

"I'd bet my life on it."

"How can you be so certain?"

"Because I remember that I was thinking that the next day, the first of September, Gargano was supposed to pay me my interest, when all of a sudden I saw his car. And I was astonished."

"Excuse me, sir, but were you, too, a victim of Gargano's?"

"Yes, I was stupid enough to have believed him. Thirty million lire, he snatched from me. But at that moment, when I saw his car, I was surprised, yes, but I was also pleased. I thought it meant he would keep his word. Whereas the next morning I was told he never showed up."

"Why were you surprised to see his car?"

"For many reasons. First of all, the place. You'll be surprised too when we get there. It's called Punta Pizzillo. Then, the hour. It was surely past midnight."

"Did you check?"

"No, I don't wear a watch. During the day I go by the sun; at night, I go by the smell of the night. I have my own sort of natural timekeeper, built into my body."

"Did you say the smell of the night?"

"Yes. The night changes smells, depending on the hour."

Montalbano didn't press him on it. He said:

"Maybe Gargano was with someone; maybe they wanted to be alone."

"Inspector Montalbano, this place is too isolated to be safe. Don't you remember that a young couple were assaulted here two years ago? And I wondered: With all the money he's got, the standing, the need to keep up appearances, what need does Gargano have to be screwing in his car like a common punk?"

"May I ask you — you're perfectly free not to answer — what you were doing in a

176

place you tell me is so isolated, at that time of the night?"

"I go walking at night."

Montalbano refrained from asking any more questions. Some five minutes later, after a spell of silence, the schoolteacher said:

"Here we are. This is Punta Pizzillo."

And he got out first, followed by the inspector. They were on a small plateau, a kind of ship's bow, utterly deserted and devoid of trees, with only a few clumps of sorghum and caper here and there. The edge of the plateau was about ten yards away; beyond it must have been a sheer drop down to the sea.

Montalbano took a few steps but was stopped by Tommasino's voice.

"Careful. There are landslides here. The ground's soft. Gargano's car was parked where yours is now, and in the same position, with the trunk facing the sea."

"And what direction were you coming from?"

"From Vigàta."

"That's far."

"Not as far as it seems. From here to Vigàta on foot, it takes forty-five minutes, an hour at the most. So, coming from that direction, I had no choice but to pass in front of the car's nose, about five or six paces away. Unless I were to make a long detour inward to avoid it. But what reason would I have to do that? And so I recognized the car. There was sufficient moonlight."

"Did you manage to get a look at the license plate?"

"Are you kidding? I would have had to stick my nose right up to it to read it."

"But if you couldn't see the license plate, how could you —"

"I recognized the model. It was an Alfa 166. The same car he was driving when he came to my house to steal my money."

"What kind of car do you drive?" the inspector thought to ask him.

"Me? I don't even have a driver's license."

Nottata persa e figlia femmina, Montalbano thought to himself, disappointed. This Tommasino was a madman who saw things that weren't there; but even when he saw things that were there, he adjusted them to his liking. The wind turned colder, the sky had clouded over. What was the inspector doing wasting his time in this godforsaken place? The schoolteacher must have somehow noticed his disappointment.

"Listen, Inspector, I have an obsession."

Oh, God, another one? Montalbano got

worried. What if the guy went bonkers right then and there and started yelling that he was seeing Lucifer in person? How should he act? Pretend it's nothing? Get in his car and hightail it out of there?

"I'm obsessed with cars," Tommasino continued. "I subscribe to quite a number of Italian and foreign magazines specializing in the subject. I could probably go on a TV game show. If the theme was cars, I'm sure I'd win."

"Was there anyone inside the car?" asked the inspector, by now resigned to Tommasino's utter unpredictability.

"You see, coming from over there, as I said, I was able to observe the car in profile, so to speak, for a short spell. Then I drew near enough to see whether or not there were any silhouettes of people inside. I didn't notice any. It's possible that, seeing a shadow approach, whoever was in the car ducked down. I walked past without turning around."

"Did you hear the sound of the car being started up at any point?"

"No. But I think — and it's only an impression, mind you — that the trunk was open."

"And was there anyone near the trunk?"
"No."

Montalbano then got an idea that was so simple it was almost embarrassing.

"Mr. Tommasino, could you please take about thirty steps and then walk back towards my car, taking the same path you took that night?"

"Certainly," said Tommasino, "I like to walk."

As the schoolteacher was walking away from him, Montalbano opened the trunk and crouched down behind the car, poking his head up just enough to allow him to look through the rear-door windows and see Tommasino take the last of his thirty paces and turn around. At that point he lowered his head, making himself completely invisible. When he figured Tommasino was in front of the car, he scrambled over behind the trunk, crouching all the while. Then he moved again to the other side of the car when he realized the schoolteacher had passed, an unnecessary precaution, since Tommasino said he hadn't turned around. At this point he stood up.

"That's enough, Mr. Tommasino, thank you."

Tommasino gave him a puzzled look.

"Where were you hiding? I saw the open trunk, but the car was empty and you were nowhere to be seen."

"You were coming from over there, and Gargano, seeing your shadow —"

He broke off. The sky had suddenly opened an eye. A small hole, a rent, had appeared in the uniformly black fabric of clouds, and through the breach a bright ray of sunlight shone down, almost entirely circumscribed, on the spot where they were standing. Montalbano felt like laughing. They looked like two characters in a naïf votive painting, illuminated by divine light. And at that moment he noticed something that only that particular angle of light, like a floodlight in a theater, could have brought to his attention. He felt a chill run down his spine, and a familiar bell began to ring in his head.

"Let me drive you home," he said to Tommasino, who was looking at him questioningly, waiting for him to continue his explanation.

After dropping off the former schoolteacher — having barely restrained himself from embracing the man — he raced back to the place they'd just been. Meanwhile no other cars had shown up to give him any trouble. He pulled up, got out, and began to walk very slowly, step by careful step, looking down at the ground all the while, as far as the edge of the cliff. The ray of sunlight was no longer there to help him like the beam of a flashlight in the night. But now he knew what he needed to look for.

Then he cautiously leaned forward to see what was under his feet. The plateau was made up of a layer of earth atop a base of marl. Below, a smooth white wall of marl plunged straight into the sea, which must have been at the very least thirty feet deep in that spot. The water was dark gray, like the sky. He didn't want to waste any more time. He looked around once, twice, thrice, to establish a few fixed reference points, then got back in his car and sped off to the station.

Fazio wasn't there. Unexpectedly, however, Mimì was.

"Beba's father's doing better. We've decided to postpone the wedding for a month. Any new developments?"

"Yes, Mimì. Many." He told him everything. When he'd finished, Mimì sat there dumbfounded.

"What are you going to do now?" he finally said.

"I want you to find me a dinghy with a

good motor. It should take me about an hour to get to the spot, even if the weather's not the greatest."

"Look, Salvo, you're liable to get a heart attack. Put it off for a little while. The water must be ice cold today. And, sorry to say, you're not a kid anymore."

"Find me a dinghy and don't break my balls."

"Have you at least got a wet suit? An oxygen tank?"

"I should have a wet suit somewhere in the house. I've never used oxygen tanks. I can dive without them, just holding my breath."

"Salvo, you *used to* dive without them, just holding your breath. Meanwhile you've kept right on smoking all these years. You don't know what condition your lungs are in. How long do you really think you can stay underwater? Shall we say twenty seconds, just to be generous?"

"That's bullshit."

"You call smoking bullshit?"

"Gimme a break with the smoking! Of course smoking is harmful, to those who smoke. But for you, smog doesn't count, high-tension wires don't count, depleted uranium is good for the health, smoke-stacks are fine, Chernobyl has boosted farming production, fish filled with uranium — or whatever the hell it is — are better for you, dioxin is a pick-me-up, and mad cow, foot-and-mouth disease, genetically modified food, and globalization will make you live like a king. The only thing that harms and kills millions of people is secondhand smoke. You know what the new slogan's going to be in the coming years? *Keep the air clean. Do a line of coke*."

"Okay, okay. Calm down," said Mimì. "I'll find you a dinghy. But on one condition."

"What condition?"

"That you bring me along."

"To do what?"

"Nothing. I just don't want to let you go alone. I wouldn't feel right."

"Okay, then. Two o'clock, at the port. I've got to keep my stomach empty, in any case. Don't tell anyone where we're going. I mean it. If I should turn out to be wrong, the whole police department'll be razzing me."

Montalbano learned how hard it was to put on a wet suit while in a dinghy speeding over a sea that wasn't exactly calm. Mimì, at the helm, looked tense and worried.

"Getting seasick?" the inspector asked him at one point.

"No. Just sick of myself."

"Why?"

"Because every now and then I realize what a stupid shit I am to go along with some of your brilliant ideas."

This was their only exchange. They didn't resume speaking until they'd finally arrived, after many aborted attempts, in the waters in front of Punta Pizzillo, facing the headland where Montalbano had been that morning. The white rock face rose straight up out of the sea without a single spur or cavity. Mimì looked at him darkly.

"We risk crashing into that, you know," he said.

"Well, make sure we don't," was all the comfort the inspector had to offer as he began to lower himself into the water, scraping his belly against the edge of the dinghy.

"You don't look so confident yourself," said Mimì.

Montalbano glared at him, unable to bring himself to plunge into the sea. He was torn. The desire to go underwater and check to see if he'd seen right was very strong; but equally strong was the sudden impulse to drop everything. The weather, of course, didn't help: the sky was so dark that it seemed almost night, and the wind had turned very cold. At last he made up his mind, mostly because he could never allow himself to lose face in front of Augello by giving up. He released his grip.

Straightaway he found himself in darkness so total, so impenetrable, that he couldn't tell which way his body was positioned in the water. Was he vertical or horizontal? He remembered the time he'd woken up in the middle of the night, in bed, unable to make out where he was, no longer knowing where to look for the usual markers: the window, the door, the ceiling. He backed into something solid, then moved aside. He touched a viscous mass with his hand. He felt it envelop him. He struggled, and broke free. He then tried frantically to do two things: resist the absurd fear that was coming over him and grab the flashlight he had in his belt. At last he managed to turn it on. To his horror, he saw no beam of light. The thing didn't work. A strong current began to pull him downward.

Why am I always trying to pull these kinds of stunts? he asked himself in despair.

Fear turned into panic. Unable to master

it, he rocketed up to the surface, crashing his head into Augello's face, as his assistant was leaning far out over the edge of the dinghy.

"You nearly broke my nose!" said Mimì, rubbing his proboscis.

"So get out of the way," retorted the inspector, grabbing hold of the dinghy. He still couldn't see a thing. Could it possibly be night already? He could only hear his own panting.

"Why are your eyes closed?" Augello asked with concern.

Only then did the inspector realize that the whole time he'd been underwater he'd kept his eyes shut, stubbornly refusing to accept what he was doing. He opened his eyes. To double-check, he turned on the flashlight, which worked fine. He just sat there a few minutes, cursing himself, and when he felt that his heartbeat had returned to normal, he lowered himself into the water again. He felt calm now. The fright he'd had must have been due to the shock of first contact with the water. A natural reaction.

He was fifteen feet under. He aimed the light still farther down and gave a start, not believing what he saw. He turned off the flashlight, counted slowly to three, then turned it back on.

Another ten or twelve feet down, tightly wedged between the wall of marl and a white rock, was the wreck of an automobile. A surge of emotion made him expel the air in his lungs. He hurriedly swam to the surface.

"Find anything? Groupers? Mackerels?" Mimì asked sarcastically, holding a wet handkerchief to his nose.

"I hit the goddamn jackpot, Mimì. The car is down there. It either crashed or was pushed off that cliff. I was right, this morning, when I thought I saw tire tracks leading all the way to the edge. I need to go back down to check something, then we'll go home."

Mimì'd had the foresight to bring along a plastic bag with towels and an unopened bottle of whisky inside. Before asking any questions, he waited for the inspector to take off the wet suit, dry off, and get dressed. He waited still longer for his boss to attack the bottle, then attacked it himself. Finally, he asked:

"So, what'd you see twenty thousand leagues under the sea?"

"Mimì, you're being a wise guy because you don't want to admit that I've left your ass in the dust. You took this case lightly, you told me yourself, and now I've screwed you. Pass the bottle."

He took a long swig and handed the bottle to Augello, who did the same. But it was obvious that after what Montalbano had said, he didn't enjoy it quite as much.

"So what'd you see?" Mimì asked again, sheepishly.

"There's a corpse inside the car. I can't tell whose it is, he's in too bad a shape. The doors probably opened on impact, so there may be another body in the area. The trunk was also open. And you know what was in there? A motorbike. And there you have it."

"What do we do now?"

"It's not our case. So we'll inform the people in charge."

The two men who stepped out of the dinghy were undoubtedly Inspector Salvo Montalbano and Assistant Inspector Domenico "Mimì" Augello, two well-known guardians of the law. But all those who saw them were rather taken aback. Arm in arm, the two policemen staggered as they walked, softly singing to themselves "La donna è mobile."

"Huddo? Id Guannodda dare?" asked

189

the inspector, speaking as if he had a very bad cold.

"Inspector Guarnotta, you mean?"

"Yed."

"Who's calling?"

"General Jaruselski."

"I'll put him on at once," said the operator, impressed.

"Hello? This is Guarnotta. I didn't quite get who this is."

"Listen, Idpector, listen clodely and don't athk eddy quedshons."

It was a long and tortuous conversation, but in the end Inspector Guarnotta of Montelusa Central Police understood that he'd received some very important information from an unknown Pole.

It was seven in the evening, and at the station no one had seen hide or hair of Fazio. Montalbano rang up his newsman friend Nicolò Zito at the Free Channel studios.

"You ever going to pick up the video Annalisa made for you?" said Zito.

"What video?"

"The one with the pieces on Gargano."

He'd forgotten completely about it, but pretended that that was the reason he'd called.

"If I drop by in half an hour, will you be there?"

When he got to the Free Channel, Zito's office door was open. The newsman was waiting for him inside, videocassette in hand.

"Come on, I'm in a hurry. I have to prepare the evening report."

"Thanks, Nicolò. I've got something to tell you: from this moment on, keep an eye on Guarnotta. Then, if you can, fill me in."

Nicolò's haste suddenly vanished. The reporter pricked up his ears, knowing that one word from Montalbano was worth more than a three-hour lecture.

"Why, is something up?"

"Yes."

"About Gargano?"

"I'd say so."

At the Trattoria San Calogero, the inspector had such an appetite that even the owner, who was used to seeing him eat, was astonished:

"What happened, Inspector, did the bottom drop out of your belly?"

He went home to Marinella, basking in genuine happiness. Not because he'd found the car. At the moment he didn't give a damn about that. But because he felt proud to know he could still engage in such demanding feats as diving without equipment.

"I'd like to see how many young guys can do what I just did!"

Old, right! How could such a gloomy thought have ever entered his head? It was too early for that!

As he was trying to insert the videocassette into the VCR, it fell to the floor. Bending down to retrieve it, he froze, unable to move, seized by a lacerating back spasm.

Old age had reared its ignoble head again.

12

It was the telephone he was hearing, not the violin of Maestro Cataldo Barbera, who'd just told him in a dream:

"Listen to this concertino."

Opening his eyes, he looked at the clock. Five to eight in the morning.

Very rarely did he wake up so late. Getting out of bed, he was pleased to note that the back pains were gone.

"Hello?"

"Hi, it's Nicolò. I'm doing a live, on-site broadcast on the eight o'clock news. Watch it."

He turned on the TV and tuned in to the Free Channel. After the opening credits, Nicolò's face appeared. In a few words he said that he was at Punta Pizzillo, thanks to a telephone tip that Montelusa Police had received from a Polish admiral concerning a car that had fallen into the sea. Inspector Guarnotta had had the brilliant intuition that it might be the Alfa 166 of the missing financier Emanuele Gargano. He therefore wasted no time arranging to have the vehicle dredged from the water, an operation that had not yet been completed. Here there was a cut. The camera, zooming vertiginously down from above, showed a small stretch of sea at the bottom of the cliff.

The car, explained Zito, off camera, was down there, some thirty feet beneath the surface, literally trapped between the wall of marl and a large rock. The cameraman then panned back and a huge pontoon with a crane, along with about a dozen motorboats, dinghies, and trawlers, appeared on the screen. The operation would take all day, Zito added, but the divers meanwhile had managed to free a corpse from the wreck and bring it to the surface. Cut. A body lying on the deck of a fishing boat, a man crouching beside it. This was Dr. Pasquano.

A reporter's voice: "Excuse me, Doctor, in your opinion, did the man die in the fall or was he murdered beforehand?"

Pasquano (barely looking up): "Get the [*bleep*] out of my face —"

The usual grace and charm.

"Now let's hear what the men in charge of the investigation have to say," said Nicolò.

They appeared all huddled together as in

194

a family photo taken outside: Commissioner Bonetti-Alderighi, Public Prosecutor Tommaseo, Chief of Forensics Arquà, and the head of the investigation, Inspector Guarnotta. All smiling as if at a picnic, all perilously close to the fragile edge of the cliff. Montalbano banished the wicked thought that had come into his head. All the same, seeing the commissioner of Montelusa Police vanish live on camera would certainly have made an unusual spectacle, to say the least.

The commissioner thanked everyone, from God in Heaven to the bailiff, for the efficiency and dispatch they'd demonstrated in carrying out . . . etc. Prosecutor Tommaseo asserted that all possibility of there being any sexual motive for the crime must be ruled out, and therefore he couldn't care less about the whole affair. Actually, he didn't really say the last part of that sentence, but he clearly implied it in his facial expression. Vanni Arquà, chief of forensics, let it be known that, at a glance, the car must have been in the water for over a month. The one who spoke most was Guarnotta, but this was only because Zito, like a good reporter, realized that the broadcast was going to the dogs and that it was up to him to ask the right questions to make the best of a bad situation.

"Inspector Guarnotta, has the body discovered inside the car been identified with any certainty?"

"No official identification has been made yet, but I think we can say that, in all probability, the body belongs to Giacomo Pellegrino."

"Was he alone in the car?"

"It's impossible to say. There was only the one body inside, but we can't rule out that there might have been another person who was thrown out of the car upon the vehicle's impact with the water. Our divers are actively searching the whole area."

"And might this second person have been Emanuele Gargano?"

"Possibly."

"Was Giacomo Pellegrino still alive when the car fell into the sea, or was he murdered beforehand?"

"That's what the autopsy will tell us. But, you see, it's not absolutely certain that we're dealing with a crime here. It might have just been an unfortunate accident. The land around here, you see, is very —"

He wasn't able to finish his sentence. The cameraman, who'd already panned out, managed to capture the scene. Behind the group, a broad strip of land collapsed and fell into the sea. As in a well-choreographed ballet, everyone shouted and leapt forward in unison. Montalbano half jumped from his armchair, as he often did when watching adventure films like *Raiders of the Lost Ark*. When they were all on safer ground, Zito resumed the interview.

"Did you find anything else inside the car?"

"We haven't had a chance yet to search the whole inside of the car. But very near the car we recovered a motorbike."

Montalbano pricked up his ears. But that was the end of the broadcast.

What could that last statement mean? *Very near the car?* He'd seen the motorbike in the trunk with his own two eyes. No mistake there. And so? There could only be two explanations: either some diver had removed it from where it was, maybe even without any particular reason for doing so; or Guarnotta was deliberately saying something he knew to be false. But, if the latter, for what purpose? Did Guarnotta have his own idea of things and was trying to make each detail conform to his overall conception?

The phone rang. It was Zito again.

"Did you like the broadcast?"

"Yes, Nicolò."

"Thanks for letting me screw the competition."

"Did you manage to get any sense of what Guarnotta's thinking?"

"That was no problem, because Guarnotta doesn't hide what he's thinking. He speaks clearly. But only off the record. He thinks it's too early to make any public statements. In his opinion, Gargano stepped on some toes in the Mafia. Either directly — that is, by pocketing some mafioso's cash — or indirectly — by taking over some turf he should never have sowed or plowed."

"But where does that poor kid Pellegrino come in?"

"Pellegrino had the bad luck to be with Gargano at the wrong moment. This is still Guarnotta's theory, mind you. And so they killed them both, stuck 'em back in the car, and plunked them into the sea. Afterwards — or even before, it makes no difference — they threw the motorbike into the water as well. It's only a matter of hours, supposedly, before we find Gargano's body around the car, unless the currents have dragged it further away."

"You buy that story?"

"No."

"Why?"

"Can you tell me what Pellegrino and

Gargano were doing in that godforsaken place at that time of the night? People only go there to fuck. And as far as I know, Gargano and Pellegrino were not —"

"Well, as far as you know isn't far enough."

Nicolò made a kind of sucking sound, his breath cut short.

"Do you mean to tell me — ?"

"For further details, please come to the Vigàta Police Station at eleven a.m.," said Montalbano, faking the voice of a department store PA system.

As he was hanging up, something came to mind that forced him to get dressed and go out before he'd had a chance to wash and shave. He got to Vigàta in just a few minutes, and when in front of the office of King Midas, he finally felt a little calmer, as it was still closed. He parked the car and waited. Then, in his rearview mirror, he saw a yellow Fiat 500, a collector's item, come up behind him. The car found a parking spot a short distance ahead of him. Out of it demurely stepped Miss Mariastella Cosentino, who went and opened the front door of King Midas Associates. The inspector let a few minutes pass, then went in. Mariastella was already at her post, motionless, a statue, right hand on the telephone, awaiting a call, the one call that would never come. She was unwilling to give up. As she had no television, and possibly no friends, either, it was likely she still didn't know that Pellegrino's body and Gargano's car had been found.

"Good morning, signorina, how are you today?"

"I'm all right, thank you."

From her tone of voice the inspector could tell she was still in the dark as to recent developments. Now he had to play the card in his hand very carefully, shrewdly, otherwise Mariastella might withdraw even more than usual.

"Have you heard the news?" he began.

What? You resolve to broach the subject carefully and shrewdly, and then come out with an opening statement more brutal, direct, and banal than even Catarella could ever think up? At this rate, might as well go at it guns blazing and get it over with all at once. The only sign Mariastella gave of having heard him was to focus her gaze on the inspector. But she didn't open her mouth, didn't ask anything.

"They found Giacomo Pellegrino's body."

Jesus Christ, could we have some kind of reaction?

At last Mariastella did something to promote her from the realm of inanimate objects to the human race. She stirred, slowly removed her right hand from the telephone receiver, and joined it to her left in a gesture of prayer. Mariastella's eyes opened wide, questioning, questioning. Montalbano felt sorry for her and gave her the answer.

"He wasn't there."

Mariastella's eyes returned to normal. As though independent of the rest of her still motionless body, her right hand moved again and slowly came to rest on the telephone. She could resume her wait.

Montalbano felt a blind rage come over him. Sticking his head inside the teller's window, he found himself face-to-face with the woman.

"You know damn well he's never going to call," he hissed.

He felt like one of those dangerous snakes, the kind whose head you're supposed to crush. He bolted out of the office in a fury.

The moment he entered the station he rang up Dr. Pasquano in Montelusa.

"What do you want, Montalbano? Why are you bothering me? There haven't been any murders in your neck of the woods, far as I know," said Pasquano, with the courtesy for which he was famous.

"So Pellegrino wasn't murdered, then."

"Where'd you hear that bullshit?"

"From you, Doctor, just now. Until proved to the contrary, the place where Gargano's car was found is on my territory."

"Yes, but the investigation's not yours! It belongs to that genius Guarnotta! And for your information, you should know that the kid was killed by a gunshot to the face. Just one. At the moment, I can't and won't say any more. Buy the paper in the coming days if you want to know the results of the autopsy. Good-bye."

The telephone rang.

"Whaddo I do, pass ya the call?"

"Cat, if you don't tell me who's on the line, how can I know whether to take the call?"

"Right you are, Chief. But the problem's who's onna line wants to remain a nominus, I mean they don't wanna tell me their name."

"Put 'em on."

"Hello, Daddy?"

It was Michela Manganaro, the bitch, using her gravelly Marlene voice.

"What do you want?"

"I heard the news on TV this morning."

"Are you such an early riser?"

"No, but I had to pack my things. This afternoon I'm going to Palermo to take some exams. I'll be away for a little while. But I'd like to see you before I go. I have something to tell you."

"Come to the station."

"No, I'd rather not, I might run into somebody unpleasant. Let's go to that little spot in the woods that you like so much. If that's okay, meet me outside my place at twelve-thirty."

"But are you sure about that?" asked Nicolò Zito, who'd shown up at eleven on the dot. "I would never have suspected. And to think that I interviewed him three or four times."

"I watched the video," said Montalbano. "And from the way he spoke and carried himself, you wouldn't necessarily have known he was homosexual."

"You see? But who told you he was? Couldn't it just be some gossip people are spreading because —"

"No, it's from a reliable source. A woman."

"And Pellegrino, too?"

"Yes."

"And do you think there was anything between them?"

"So I'm told."

Nicolò Zito pondered this for a moment.

"That doesn't really change things, however, not in any significant way. They might have been partners in the scam."

"It's possible. I merely wanted to tell you to keep your eyes open, since the situation may not be so simple as Guarnotta would have it. And another thing: Try to find out exactly where they found the motorbike."

"Guarnotta said —"

"I know what Guarnotta said. What I need to know is whether this corresponds to reality. Because if the motorbike was found a short distance away from the car, it means one of the divers moved it from where it was."

"And where was it?"

"In the trunk."

"How do you know that?"

"I saw it."

Nicolò looked at him, flabbergasted.

"*You* are the Polish admiral?"

"I never said I was Polish or an admiral," Montalbano solemnly declared.

A bitch, yes, but a beautiful bitch, even more beautiful than the time before, perhaps because she was over her flu. She climbed into the car, thighs flashing festively in the wind. Montalbano turned onto the second road on the right, then took the dirt road on the left.

"You remember the road very well. Did you come back here afterward, by any chance?" asked Michela as the wood came into view, opening her mouth for the first time.

"I have a good memory," said Montalbano. "What did you want to see me about?"

"C'mon, what's the hurry?" said the girl.

She stretched like a cat, wrists crossed over her head, bust arching backwards. Her blouse looked like it was about to burst.

A bra probably feels like a straitjacket to her, the inspector thought.

"Cigarette."

As he was lighting it for her, he asked:

"What exams are you going to be taking?"

Michela laughed so heartily she started coughing on the smoke of her cigarette.

"I might take one if I have any time left."

"If you've any time left? What else are you going to do?"

Michela merely stared at him, eyes twinkling with amusement. Her expression was more eloquent than a long and detailed speech. Furious, the inspector felt himself blushing. Without warning, he wrapped his right arm around Michela's shoulders, squeezed her tightly against him, brutally sliding his other hand between her legs.

"Let me go! Let me go!" the girl cried in a suddenly shrill, almost hysterical voice. Breaking free of the inspector's embrace, she opened the car door. She was genuinely upset and irritated. She got out of the car but did not walk away. Montalbano, who hadn't moved from his seat, glared at her. Out of the blue, Michela broke into a smile, reopened the car door, and sat back down beside the inspector.

"You're a shrewd one," she said. "I guess I fell for your little charade. I should have let you go on, just to see how you would have wiggled out of it."

"I'd have wiggled out the same way as last time," said Montalbano, "when you got the bright idea to kiss me. But, anyway, I knew you'd react that way. Do you really enjoy being such a tease?"

"Yes. The same way you enjoy playing the prude. Peace?"

The girl had it all, including a good dose of intelligence.

"Peace," said Montalbano. "Did you really want to tell me something or was it just an excuse to have some fun?"

"A little of both," said Michela. "I was pretty shaken this morning, when I heard Giacomo was dead. Do you know how he died?"

"Shot once in the face."

The girl gave a start, then two tears as big as pearls wet her blouse.

"I'm sorry, I need some air."

She got out of the car. As she was walking away, Montalbano saw her shoulders heave with her sobbing. Which reaction was more normal, hers or Mariastella's? All things considered, both were normal. He also got out, then walked up to the girl, offering her a handkerchief.

"The poor guy! I feel so bad!" said Michela, wiping her eyes.

"Were you close friends?"

"No, but we worked together in the same room for two years. Isn't that enough?" Her proper Italian was starting to break down into dialect. "Can you hold me?"

For a second Montalbano didn't understand the question. Then he put his arm around her shoulders. Michela leaned against him.

"Do you want to go back in the car?"

"No. It's the fact it was his face that. . . . He cared so much about his face . . . shaved twice a day . . . used skin creams . . . I'm sorry, I know I'm just babbling, but . . ."

She sniffled. Jesus, she was so much more beautiful this way!

"I didn't really understand the bit about the motorbike," she said, getting hold of herself after taking a deep breath.

The inspector tensed, paying close attention.

"The people in charge of the investigation say they found it underwater, near Gargano's car," said Montalbano. "Why do you mention it?"

"Because they used to put it in the trunk."

"Explain."

"Well, at least that's what they did once, when Gargano asked Giacomo to come with him to Montelusa. Since he couldn't drive him back because he had to go somewhere else afterward, they stuck the motorbike in the trunk, which was very spacious. That way Giacomo could come back by himself whenever he wanted."

"Maybe when the car struck the rock, the trunk opened up and the motorbike fell out."

"Maybe," said Michela. "But there are lot of things I just don't get."

"Such as?"

"I'll tell you on the way back. I want to go home."

As they were getting back in the car, the inspector remembered that someone else had used the same words as Michela: "a spacious trunk."

13

"There are lots of things that don't make sense to me," said Michela, as the inspector drove slowly back to town. "First of all, why was Gargano's car found around here? There are two possibilities: Either the last time he was down here he left it with Giacomo, or else he came back. But to do what? If he was planning to disappear after tucking the money away in a safe place — which he certainly was, since the usual transfer of funds from Bologna to Vigàta was never made that last time — then why did he come and risk losing everything?"

"Go on."

"Also, assuming Gargano was with Giacomo, why meet in the car like a couple of secret lovers? Why not meet at Gargano's hotel or in some other quiet, safe place? I'm sure all the other times they got together it wasn't in Gargano's car. It's true that Gargano was cheap, but —"

"How do you know Gargano was cheap?"

"Well, cheap cheap, maybe not, but he

was certainly tight. I know because I went out to dinner with him one night, actually twice —"

"He asked you out?"

"Of course. It was part of his seduction strategy. He enjoyed it. Anyway, he took me to a trattoria in Montelusa, and I could tell from his expression that he was afraid I might order expensive dishes. And then he complained when the bill came."

"You said it was part of his strategy. Don't you think it was because you're beautiful? I think all men like to be seen with a girl like you at their side."

"Thanks for the compliment. I don't want to seem mean, but I have to tell you he also took Mariastella out to dinner. And the next day Mariastella was in a complete daze, a beatific smile on her face, not knowing if she was coming or going, walking around the office knocking into furniture. And you know something?"

"Tell me."

"Mariastella reciprocated. She invited him to dinner at her place. And Gargano went, or so I gathered, at least, since Mariastella didn't say anything but merely cooed with contentment, lost in the clouds."

"Does she have a nice house?"

"I've never been there. It's big house, a villa, just outside Vigàta, pretty isolated. She used to live there with her parents. Now she's all alone."

"Is it true that Mariastella keeps on paying the rent and telephone bills for the office?"

"Absolutely."

"Does she have money?"

"Her father must have left her something. You know what? She wanted to pay me, out of her own pocket, for the two missing paychecks. 'The *ragioniere* will reimburse me later,' she said. Actually, no. In fact, she blurted out, 'Emanuele will reimburse me later,' and then turned red as a beet. She's just crazy about the man and doesn't want to accept reality."

"And what's the reality?"

"That in the best of cases, Gargano's living it up on some Polynesian island. And in the worst, he's being eaten up by the fish in the sea."

They arrived. Michela gave Montalbano a kiss on the cheek and got out. Then she leaned into the open window and said:

"Actually I have three exams to take in Palermo."

"Good luck," said Montalbano. "Let me know how it goes."

He went straight home to Marinella. As soon as he stepped inside, he noticed that Adelina had returned to work. The linen and shirts were on the bed, ironed and folded. He opened the refrigerator and found it empty, except for some black olives, fresh anchovies dressed in olive oil, vinegar, and oregano, and a generous slice of caciocavallo cheese. His mild disappointment vanished when he opened the oven: inside was a casserole of the legendary *pasta 'ncasciata!* Four servings' worth. Slowly and with perseverance, he shoveled it all down. Then, since the weather permitted, he settled himself in on the veranda. He needed to think. But he didn't do any thinking. Before long, the sound of the surf gently lulled him to sleep.

Good thing I'm not a crocodile, or I'd drown in my own tears.

This was the last meaningful, or meaningless, thought that came into his head.

By four he was back in his office, and Mimì immediately popped in.

"Where were you?" the inspector asked him.

"Out doing my job. As soon as I heard

the news, I rushed to the scene and made myself available to Guarnotta. On your behalf, according to our commissioner's guidelines. That's our turf, isn't it? Did I do the right thing?"

When he put his mind to it, Augello could show them all a thing or two.

"Absolutely. Well done."

"I told him I was only there in a supporting role. If he wanted, I would even go buy cigarettes for them. He was very appreciative."

"Did they find Gargano's body?"

"No, and they're discouraged. They consulted a fisherman from the area, and he told them that unless Gargano's been held up by some rock, by this point, with all the strong currents they've got around there, that body's already sailing to Tunisia. So, if they don't find anything by tonight, they're going to stop looking."

Fazio appeared in the doorway. The inspector signaled to him to come in and sit down. Fazio had a solemn look on his face. It was obvious he could barely hold himself back.

"And so?" Montalbano asked Mimì.

"So Guarnotta's scheduled a press conference for tomorrow morning."

"Know what he's going to say?"

"Of course. Why else do you think I dashed all the way out to that horrible place? He's going to say that both Gargano and Pellegrino are victims of a vendetta by the Mafia, which our *ragioniere* had taken for a ride."

"But how, I ask you, could this blessed Mafia have possibly known a day in advance that Gargano was going to bail out on his commitments, and then killed him? If they'd killed him on the first or second of September, I would understand. But to kill him the day before, doesn't that seem just a little teeny bit odd to you?"

"Of course it seems odd to me. Extremely odd. But don't ask me, ask Guarnotta."

The inspector, smiling broadly, turned to Fazio.

"And where have you been hiding yourself?"

"I'm packing," said Fazio, dead serious. "Big guns."

What he meant was that he had some high cards to play. Montalbano asked him no questions, letting Fazio take his time and savor his achievement. Fazio took a little piece of paper out of his pocket, consulted it, and resumed speaking.

"I succeeded in finding out what I

wanted to know, and it cost me a lot."

"Did you have to pay?" asked Augello.

Fazio shot him an annoyed glance.

"I meant it cost me a lot of talk and patience. Banks refuse to give information on their clients' little business ventures, especially when these ventures have a bad smell about them. But I managed to talk an official into spilling the beans anyway. He got down on his knees and asked me not to repeat his name. Are we in agreement on that?"

"Yes," said Montalbano. "Especially since this is isn't our case. We're acting out of pure and simple curiosity. Call it private curiosity."

"So," said Fazio. "On the first of October of last year, at the bank where he deposited his monthly paycheck, a wire transfer of two hundred million lire was credited to the account of Giacomo Pellegrino. A second transfer of the same amount came in on the fifteenth of January of this year. The last such transfer, this time for three hundred million, was made on the seventh of July. Seven hundred million lire in all. Pellegrino didn't have any other accounts at any other bank in Vigàta or Montelusa."

"Who was wiring these transfers?" asked Montalbano.

"Emanuele Gargano."

"Wow," said Augello.

"But from the bank where he kept his personal account, not the one he used for King Midas," Fazio continued. "Therefore the money sent to Pellegrino had nothing to do with Midas's business dealings. It was clearly a personal matter."

When Fazio had finished speaking, he was wearing a long face. He was disappointed that Montalbano showed no surprise. The information seemed to have left the inspector indifferent. Fazio, however, refused to give up and tried again.

"And you want to know something else I discovered? Every time he received a new transfer of funds, the next day Pellegrino would turn the money over to —"

"— to the construction company building his house," Montalbano concluded.

There's an old story that tells how, once upon a time, the king of France, sick and tired of hearing his wife, the queen of France, tell him he didn't love her because he never got jealous, asked a gentleman of the court to come into the queen's bedchamber the following morning, throw himself at her royal feet, and pledge his undying love to her. The king would then barge in a few minutes later and, seeing what was transpiring, throw a terrible jealous fit in front of his wife. And so the following morning the king took up position behind the queen's door, waited for the courtier to come in, counted to one hundred, unsheathed his sword, and burst into the room. But what he saw were the queen and courtier, naked on the bed, fucking with such gusto that they didn't even notice he'd come in. The poor king left the room, put the sword back in its sheath, and said: "Damn! They ruined my scene!"

Fazio did exactly the opposite of the king of France. Seeing Montalbano ruin his scene, he bolted out of his chair, turned bright red, cursed, and stormed out of the room, muttering to himself.

"What's with him?" asked Augello, surprised.

"The fact is that sometimes I'm kind of a jerk," said Montalbano.

"You're telling me!" said Augello, himself a frequent victim of Montalbano's jerkiness.

Fazio returned almost immediately. One could see he'd gone out to wash his face.

"Sorry about that," he said.

"No, I'm the one who's sorry," the inspector replied in all sincerity. Then he continued: "So the villa was entirely paid for by Gargano. The only question is: Why?"

Mimì opened his mouth, but a gesture from the inspector made him close it again.

"I first want to know if I'm remembering something correctly," said Montalbano, turning to Fazio. "Was it you who told me that when Pellegrino rented a car in Montelusa he specified that he wanted one with a spacious trunk?"

"Yes," said Fazio.

"And at the time we thought it was for his suitcases?"

"Yes."

"Which was incorrect, because he left his suitcases at his new house."

"Then what did he want to put in the trunk?" Augello cut in.

"His motorbike. He rented the car in Montelusa, put his motorbike in the trunk, drove out to Punta Raisi to do his little number with the airplane tickets, drove back to Montelusa, turned in the rented car, and came back to Vigàta on his motorbike."

"That doesn't seem very important to me," Mimì commented.

"It is, in fact, very important. Because I've learned, among other things, that he'd once put his motorbike in the trunk of Gargano's car."

"Okay, but —"

"Let's forget the motorbike for a moment. Let's return to the question of why Gargano paid for the construction of Pellegrino's new house. Bear in mind that I've also learned — and I trust my source — that Gargano was a tightwad, always careful not to waste any money."

Augello spoke first.

"Why couldn't it have been for love? From what you've told me yourself, there was more than just sex between them."

"What do you think?" Montalbano asked Fazio.

"Inspector Augello's explanation could be right. But, and I can't really say why, I'm not convinced. I would lean more towards blackmail."

"Blackmail over what?"

"I dunno, maybe Pellegrino threatened to tell everyone they had a relationship — that Gargano was gay . . ."

Augello burst out laughing. Fazio gave him a puzzled look.

"Come on, Fazio! How old are you? Nowadays, thank God, nobody gives a shit if you're gay or not!"

"Gargano made a point of not letting it show," Montalbano cut in. "But I don't think it would have been such a big deal even if there had been some danger of the fact becoming known. No, that sort of threat would not have made someone like Gargano succumb to blackmail."

Fazio threw his hands up and stopped defending his hypothesis. Then he stared at the inspector. Augello, too, started staring at him.

"What's wrong with you two?"

"What's wrong with us is that it's your turn to talk," said Mimì.

"All right," said the inspector. "But let me preface this by saying that what I'm about to describe is a novel. In the sense that there isn't the slightest trace of proof for any of it. And, as in all novels, as the story gets written, events sometimes go their own way, leading to unforeseen conclusions."

"Okay," said Augello.

"We begin with something we know for certain: Gargano organizes a scam that, by definition, cannot be pulled off over the course of a week, but requires a long time to develop. Not only: he also needs to set up a genuine business with offices, employees, and so on. Among the employees he hires in Vigàta is a kid named Giacomo Pellegrino. After a while, the two begin to have an affair. They sort of fall in love; it's not just a one-night stand. The person who told me this added that, though they tried to hide it, their relationship became visible in their behavior. Some days they'd smile at each other and seek each other out, while other days they'd pout and snub each other. Exactly the way lovers do. Isn't that how it is, Mimì? You know about these things, don't you?"

"Why, you don't?"

"The point is," Montalbano continued, "you're both right. Their story begins in ambiguity and is played out in ambiguity. Pellegrino is one of those partial intelligences that —"

"Stop right there," said Mimì. "What does that mean?"

"By partial intelligence I mean the intelligence of someone who works in money. Not in farming, business, industry, construction, or what have you, but in money for its own sake. These people know or sense everything there is to know about money, every hour, every minute of the day. They know it as well as they know themselves. They know how it pissed today, how it shat, ate, and slept, how it woke up this morning. They know its good days and its bad days, they know when it wants to give birth — that is, when it wants to produce more money — or when it's contemplating suicide, when it wants to remain sterile, and even when it wants to have sex without commitments. They know when it will take off, they know when it will go into free fall, as the specialists on the TV news like to put it. These partial intelligences are called things like financial wizards, big bankers, big brokers, big speculators. Their brains, however, function only on that one wavelength. In every other respect they're ill equipped, awkward, limited, backward, even downright stupid. But never naïve."

"Your portrait seems a little excessive to me," said Augello.

"Oh, yeah? And in your opinion that guy who was found hanged under the Blackfriars' Bridge in London wasn't a partial intelligence? How about that other guy, the one who faked being kidnapped by the Mafia, shot himself in the leg, and then drank a cup of poisoned coffee in prison? Give me a break!"

Mimì didn't dare contradict him.

"To return to Giacomo Pellegrino," said

Montalbano. "He's a partial intelligence who meets up with an even more partial intelligence, that is, the *ragioniere* Emanuele Gargano, who senses their elective affinity right off the bat. So he hires him and begins to assign him various tasks that he's careful not to give to his other two employees. Then the relationship between Gargano and Pellegrino changes; they discover that their elective affinity is not limited to money, but can be extended as well to the emotional sphere. I said these people are never naïve, but there are always different levels of naïveté. Let's just say that Giacomo is a little shrewder than Gargano. But this slight difference is more than enough for the kid."

"In what sense?" asked Augello.

"In the sense that Giacomo must have discovered almost immediately that there was something going on at King Midas that didn't add up. But he kept it to himself, with the intention, however, of carefully following every move and transaction his employer made. So he starts compiling data, and begins to connect the dots. And maybe, in their more intimate moments, he even asks a few questions that appear to be off-handed but which actually have a precise goal in mind, which is to work his way further and further into Gargano's schemes."

"And Gargano's so in love with the kid that he never gets suspicious?" Fazio interjected with a tone of skepticism.

"You hit the nail on the head," said the inspector. "And this is the most delicate point in the novel we're writing. Let's see if we can understand how the Gargano character acts. Remember that at the beginning I said their relationship was marked by ambiguity. I am convinced that at some point Gargano sensed that Giacomo was getting dangerously close to understanding the workings of his scam. But what can he do? Firing him would make things worse. So he plays the fool, as the saying goes, to avoid going to war."

"So he hopes Pellegrino will be satisfied with the gift of the house and won't ask for anything else?" inquired Mimì.

"Yes, in a way, because he's not sure whether Giacomo is blackmailing him or not. The kid probably persuaded him by insisting how wonderful it would be to have their own love nest, a place where they could even go and live together after Gargano retires. . . . He probably set his mind at rest this way. But they both know — though they never let on — how the whole thing will end. Gargano will flee abroad with the money, and Giacomo, not being in any way involved in the scam, can enjoy his new house in peace."

"I still can't understand why he told his uncle he was leaving for Germany," said Fazio as if to himself.

"Because he knew the uncle would tell us once we started looking for Gargano; meanwhile we were supposed to sit around waiting for him to return before investigating any further. Then he would finally turn up, innocent as a baby, and tell us that, yes, he'd been to Germany, but it had all been a trick on Gargano's part to get him out of the way, since he was the only person who might understand, in time, that Gargano was about to haul in the nets. He would tell us that no money had ever been wired to the banks where Gargano had sent him."

"So then why go through the whole song and dance of the plane tickets?" Fazio insisted.

"To protect himself, just in case. Protect himself from everyone: from Gargano and from us. Believe me, Giacomo planned it all very carefully. But then the unexpected happened."

"What?" asked Mimì.

"Is a bullet in the face unexpected enough for you?" said the inspector.

14

"Shall we continue tomorrow with part two? You know, I'm beginning to realize as I go along that, more than a novel, this is a TV script. If I'd written and published this novel, that's probably what some reviewer would have said about it, adding something like 'Yes, a TV script, and not a particularly good one.' So, what now?"

Montalbano's suggestion elicited protests from his two listeners. He certainly couldn't complain about his audience ratings. He was forced to go on, after having asked for, and been granted, a brief coffee break.

"Lately, however, Gargano's and Pellegrino's relationship appears to be deteriorating," he resumed, "though we can't know this with any certainty."

"We could," asserted Augello.

"How?"

"By asking the same person who gave you all the other information."

"I don't know where she is. She's gone to Palermo."

"Then ask Miss Cosentino."

"That I could do. But she never caught on to anything, even when Gargano and Pellegrino were necking right under her nose."

"Okay. Let's assume their relationship deteriorated. Why?"

"I didn't say it deteriorated, I said it appeared to be deteriorating."

"What's the difference?" asked Fazio.

"The difference is a big one. If they're quarreling in front of everyone, if they're acting cold and distant to each other, it's because they've agreed in advance to do so. It's all a put-on."

"That seems a little far-fetched, even for a TV movie made from a novel," Mimì said sarcastically.

"If you want, we can cut those scenes from the script. But that would be a mistake. You see, I think the kid, when he sees that the scam is drawing to its conclusion, decides to make his blackmail explicit. He wants to get the most out of it before Gargano disappears. So he asks for more money. Gargano, however, won't fork it over, and this we know for a fact because you, Fazio, said that there were no more deposits made. And what does the *ragioniere* do then, knowing that a blackmailer's hunger is never satisfied? He pretends to give in, and he even ups the ante, making the kid an offer while declaring his undying love for him in spite of everything. He says they'll run away together with the money and live happily ever after in some foreign country. Giacomo, deep down, doesn't trust him, but he accepts on one condition: Gargano must tell him in which foreign banks the King Midas money was deposited.

"Gargano gives him the names, along with all the access codes, and at the same time tells him that it would be better if they pretended to have a falling out in front of the others, that way when the police start looking for him after the scam is discovered, they won't have any reason to think they fled together. And for the same reason, says Gargano, they should arrive at their foreign destination separately. They may have even chosen the city where they would meet."

"Now I understand Gargano's game!" Mimì interjected. "He actually gave Giacomo the real access codes to the accounts. The kid checks them and is able to see that the *ragioniere* is not setting a trap for him. Whereas in fact Gargano is planning to transfer the money somewhere else just a few hours before making his getaway, since nowadays you can do these things in a matter of minutes. And he's also planning not to show up for their appointment in that foreign city."

"Right on the mark, Mimì. But we've established that our little Giacomo is no fool in these matters. He's wise to Gargano's plan and keeps him under surveillance with his cellphone, calling him nonstop. Then, when the moment comes — that is, when the thirty-first of August arrives — he calls Gargano at the crack of dawn and, threatening to tell the whole story to the police, he forces him to come straight to Vigàta. Which means that they'll skip the country together, says Giacomo. He's willing to risk it. Gargano at this point knows he has no choice. He gets in his car and leaves, not using his highway pass, so as not to leave any tracks. He arrives at the appointed place. It's already night. Giacomo shows up a little later on his motorbike, which he's been keeping at his new house. He doesn't give a damn about the two big suitcases anymore; the important thing is the briefcase, in which he's carrying the proof of the scam. So the two men meet."

"Can I tell the rest?" Fazio butted in.

And he continued: "They have an argument. Gargano at this point knows he's done for, since the kid's got him in the palm of his hand, so he whips out the pistol and shoots him."

"In the face," adds Augello, to be precise.

"Is that so important?"

"Yes. When somebody shoots somebody in the face, it's almost always out of hatred, like they want to blot them out."

"I don't think there was any argument," said Montalbano. "On his drive down from Bologna, Gargano had all the time he needed to think about the dangerous predicament he was in, and to reach the conclusion that the kid had to go. I realize, of course, that a violent scuffle, preferably at the edge of the cliff, with first one, then the other protagonist in danger of falling off, with Giacomo trying to disarm Gargano and a raging sea in the background, might work well on TV, if you could come up with the right musical soundtrack as commentary. Unfortunately I think Gargano shot Giacomo as soon as he saw him. He didn't have any time to lose."

"So in your opinion he killed him outside the car?"

"Of course. Then he grabbed him and

put him behind the steering wheel. But the body probably slid to one side, so he laid it down over the two seats. That's why when Tommasino walked by he didn't see the body and thought the car was empty. Gargano then opens the trunk, pulls out his suitcase — which he probably brought along for good measure, as a prop, in case he needed to show that he was ready to leave — then puts the motorbike in its place, not forgetting, of course, to remove the briefcase with the documents from the bike's little baggage box. His own suitcase he puts in the backseat of the car. This is when Tommasino shows up. Gargano plays hide-and-seek with the schoolteacher, waits till he's a safe distance away, closes the car's doors, and proceeds to push the vehicle off the edge of the cliff. He's imagining — correctly, I might add — that some idiot will start looking for his body, convinced that the whole crime is a vendetta on the part of the Mafia. Briefcase in hand, he begins walking, and in less than half an hour he's on a road with cars driving by. He hitches a ride with somebody, whom he probably pays handsomely not to talk."

"I'll finish," said Mimì. "Final shot. Music. We see a long, straight road —"

"Are there any in Sicily?" asked Montalbano.

"It doesn't matter. We film the scene on the mainland and pretend, with a little montage, that it's here. The car drives farther and farther away, till it becomes a tiny little dot. The frame freezes. On the screen appear the words: 'And thus evil triumphs and the forces of justice get fucked.' Credits."

"I don't like that ending," Fazio said very seriously.

"I don't either," Montalbano chimed in. "But you'll have to resign yourself, Fazio. That's exactly the way it is. Justice, nowadays, can go fuck itself. Bah. Let's forget about it."

Fazio scowled even more grimly.

"But is there really nothing we can do to get Gargano?"

"Go tell our screenplay to Guarnotta and see what he says."

Fazio got up and was about to leave the room when he ran straight into Catarella, who was rushing in, out of breath and palefaced.

"Ohmygod, Chief! The c'mishner just called just now! Ohmygod, what a scare he gives me whenever he calls!"

"Did he want me?"

"No, Chief."

"Who'd he want, then?"

"Me, Chief, me! Ohmygod, I'm feelin' all weak in the knees-like! Can I sit down?"

"Sit down, Cat. Why'd he want you?"

"Well, it happened like so. The tiliphone rings. I pick up and answer h'lo. And then I hear the c'mishner's voice. 'Is that you, Santarella?' he says. 'Poissonally in poisson,' I says. 'I want you to tell something to the inspector,' he says. 'He ain't here,' I says, 'cause I knew you dint feel like talking to him. 'That doesn't matter,' he says. 'Tell him I acknowledge receipt.' An' he hangs up. Inspector, what's this receipt the c'mishner's talking about? I don't know anything about any receipt!"

"Skip it, don't worry about it. And relax."

Was the c'mishner trying to offer him peace with honor? If so, the c'mishner would have to ask for it straight out. Offering it wasn't enough.

Back home at Marinella, he found the sweater Livia had given him on the table, and beside it a note from Adelina saying that, having come by in the afternoon to clean up the house, she'd found the sweater on top of the armoire. She added that, having found some nice hake at the market, she'd boiled a few of them for him.

He needed only add oil, lemon, and salt.

What to do with the sweater? God, was it ever hard to hide a corpus delicti! He thought he'd got that sweater safely out of the way; it could have remained for all eternity where he'd thrown it. And yet here it was again. The only solution was to bury it in the sand. But he felt tired. So he grabbed the sweater and flung it back where it had been before. It was unlikely that Adelina in the coming days would sniff it out again. The telephone rang. It was Nicolò, telling him to turn on the television. There was going to be a special edition of the news at nine-thirty. He looked at his watch. Nine-fifteen. He went into the bathroom, got undressed, washed himself quickly, then settled into the armchair. He would eat the hake after the news.

After the opening credits, an image that looked like something out of an American movie appeared. A large, mangled automobile rose slowly out of the water as Zito's voice-over explained that this difficult dredging operation had taken place shortly before sunset. Next they showed the car resting on the deck of a pontoon while some men freed it from the steel cables with which it had been hoisted. Then Guarnotta's face appeared.

"Inspector Guarnotta, could you please tell us what you found inside Mr. Gargano's car?"

"In the backseat we found a suitcase containing Gargano's personal effects."

"Anything else?"

"Nothing else."

This confirmed that the *ragioniere* had taken Giacomo's precious briefcase away with him.

"Are you going to continue to search for Gargano's body?"

"I can officially announce that the search for Gargano has ended. We're more than convinced that his body was dragged out to sea by the current."

And this proved that Gargano had been right in his calculations. There had indeed been an idiot ready to believe the whole setup. There he was, the illustrious Inspector Guarnotta.

"There's a rumor circulating — which it is our journalistic duty to mention here — that relations between Pellegrino and Gargano were somewhat unusual. Can you confirm this?"

"We too have heard this rumor and are investigating the matter. If it proves to be true, it could be important."

"Why, Inspector?"

"Because it would explain why Gargano and Pellegrino met late at night in this secluded, seldom frequented place. They came here to — how shall I say? — to be alone. And they were followed here and killed."

It was hopeless. Guarnotta was besotted with his bugaboo. It had to be the Mafia, therefore it was the Mafia.

"About an hour ago we had a chance to talk on the phone with Dr. Pasquano, the coroner, who has just completed the autopsy on the body of Giacomo Pellegrino. He said the young man was killed by a single gunshot wound, right between the eyes, fired at close range. The bullet, which did not exit the body, has been recovered. Dr. Pasquano says it is from a small-caliber weapon."

Zito stopped, saying no more. Guarnotta looked puzzled.

"So?"

"Well, wouldn't that be a rather unusual weapon for the Mafia?"

Guarnotta chuckled condescendingly.

"The Mafia uses whatever weapon it wants. It has no preferences. From a bazooka to the tip of a toothpick. Never forget that."

Zito's face looked visibly dumbfounded. Apparently he did not understand how a toothpick could become a lethal weapon.

Montalbano turned off the television.

Among these weapons, my good Guarnotta, he said to himself, *there are also people like you. Judges, policemen, and carabinieri who see the Mafia when it's not there, and do not see it when it is.*

But he didn't want to give in to anger. The little hakes were waiting for him.

He decided to go to bed early so he could read a little. He'd just lain down when the phone rang.

"Darling? Everything's all set at this end. I'll be flying out tomorrow afternoon. I should be in Vigàta by around eight o'clock."

"If you tell me what time you get in, I'll come pick you up at Punta Raisi. I don't have much going on. I'm happy to do it."

"The fact is I've still got some hassles at the office. I don't know exactly what time I'll be able to leave. So don't worry about it, I'll just take the bus. I'll be there when you get home from work."

"Okay."

"But try to come home early, don't do as you usually do. I really want to be with you."

"Why, don't you think I do, too?"

Instinctively, his eye wandered up to the top of the armoire where the sweater lay hidden. He would have to bury it the next morning, before going to work. But what if Livia asked what had happened to her present? He would feign surprise, and thus Livia would end up suspecting Adelina, whom she detested and who repaid her in kind. Then, almost without realizing what he was doing, he grabbed a chair, pushed it against the armoire, climbed up on it, felt around with his hand until he found the sweater, seized it, stepped down from the chair, put it back, took the sweater in both hands and with great effort managed to rip it and start tearing it apart, making one, two, three holes in it; then he armed himself with a knife, stabbed it five or six times, threw it down on the ground, and began stamping on it with both feet. A genuine murderer in the throes of a homicidal frenzy. In the end he left it on the kitchen table so he would remember to bury it the following morning. And all at once he felt profoundly ridiculous. Why had he let himself succumb to such stupid, uncontrolled rage? Perhaps because he'd completely repressed it, and then lo, the sweater had so brutally reappeared before his eyes? Well, now that he'd got it out of his system, not only did he find himself ridiculous, but he fell prey to a kind of melancholy remorse. Poor Livia, who'd so lovingly chosen that very sweater as a present for him! Then an absurd, impossible comparison occurred to him. How would Mariastella Cosentino have behaved in the grips of a sweater given her by Gargano, the man she loved? Or, rather, adored — to the point that she couldn't see, or wouldn't see, that the *ragioniere* was nothing more than a rogue and con artist who'd run off with the money and who, to avoid having to share it, had murdered a man in cold blood. Why hadn't she reacted when, to calm down the old man Garzullo, he'd concocted that story about the TV announcing that Gargano'd been arrested? She had no television at home, so it seemed logical to assume that she would have believed what Montalbano said. Whereas, nothing. Not a move, not a start, not even a sigh. It was more or less the same reaction she had when he told her that Pellegrino's corpse had been found. She should have fallen into despair, imagining that her beloved *ragioniere* had suffered a similar fate. Whereas, that time, too, she'd behaved the same way. He'd felt as if he was talking to something rather like a statue with its eyes popping out. Miss Mariastella Cosentino behaved as if —

The telephone rang. Was it possible that one could never fall asleep in peace in that house? Anyway, it was late, almost one o'clock. Cursing the saints, he picked up the receiver.

"Hello? Who is this?" he asked in a voice that would have frightened a highwayman.

"Did I wake you up? It's Nicolò."

"No, I was still awake. Any news?"

"No, but I wanted to tell you something that'll cheer you up."

"I'm in need of it."

"You want to know what theory Prosecutor Tommaseo came up with in an interview I just did with him? He said it probably wasn't the Mafia that killed the two men, as Guarnotta thinks."

"So who was it, then?"

"For Tommaseo it was a third man, a jealous lover who caught them in the act. What do you think?"

"With Tommaseo, the minute there's a hint of sex, his imagination runs away with him. When are you going to broadcast it?"

"Never. When the chief prosecutor found out about it, he called me up all embarrassed, poor guy. So I gave him my word I would never make the interview public."

He read three pages of Simenon, but no

matter how hard he tried, he couldn't read any further. He was too sleepy. He turned off the light and plunged at once into a rather unpleasant dream. He was underwater again, near Gargano's car, and could see Giacomo's body inside the cab, moving about like an astronaut, weightless, and tracing what looked like a dance step. Then a voice came from the other side of the rock.

"Cuckoo! Cuckoo!"

He turned around at once and saw Emanuele Gargano — he, too, long dead, face covered with green sea moss, algae twisting around his arms and legs. The current was making his body spin slowly around, as though he were mounted on a spit and roasting. Every time Gargano's face, or what remained of it, turned upwards and faced Montalbano, the mouth opened and said:

"Cuckoo! Cuckoo!"

Tearing himself with difficulty from the dream, he woke up all covered in sweat. He turned on the light. And he had the impression that another light, violent and swift as lightning, had flashed for a moment inside his head.

He completed the sentence that Zito's phone call had interrupted: Miss Mariastella Cosentino behaved as if she knew exactly where Emanuele Gargano was hiding.

15

After that last thought, he was barely able to get any sleep. He would drift off only to wake up again less than half an hour later with Mariastella Cosentino on his mind. Of the other two King Midas employees he'd been able to get a clear sense, even though he'd never seen Giacomo except as a corpse. At seven o'clock he got up, put in the videocassette that the Free Channel had made for him, and watched it carefully. Mariastella appeared twice in it, both times during the inauguration of the Vigàta office, both times at Gargano's side, showering him with adoring glances. A love at first sight, therefore, which over time had become total, absolute. He had to speak with the woman and had a good excuse for doing so. Since his assumptions were gradually being borne out, he would ask her if relations between Gargano and Pellegrino had grown tense towards the end. If she said yes, then this assumption, too — that is, that the men had conspired to pretend they were at odds — would prove to have been correct. Yet before going to see her, he decided he needed to know more about her.

He got to headquarters around eight and immediately summoned Fazio.

"I need some information on Mariastella Cosentino."

"O Gesù biniditto!" said Fazio.

"What's so shocking about that?"

"What's shocking, Chief, is that lady might look alive, but she's really dead! What do you want to know?"

"Whether there is or was any gossip about her circulating in town. Like what she did or where she worked before Gargano hired her. And who her father and mother were. Where she lives and what her habits are. We know, for example, that she has no television, but does have a phone."

"How much time have I got?"

"Report back to me no later than eleven."

"All right, Chief, but you have to do me a favor."

"Gladly, if I can."

"You can, Chief, you can."

He went out and returned at once with half a ton of documents in his arms.

At eleven on the dot Fazio knocked on the door and came in. The inspector was pleased to see him. He'd managed to sign three-fourths of the papers, and his arm was getting stiff.

"Get these papers off my desk."

"Even the ones you haven't signed?"

"Them too."

Fazio picked them up, took them to his office, and came back.

"I didn't find out much," he said, sitting down.

He pulled from his pocket a sheet of paper densely covered with scrawl.

"Fazio, before you begin, I implore you to rein in your records office complex as much as possible. Tell me only the essentials. I don't give a shit about where and when Mariastella's parents were married. Okay?"

"Okay," said Fazio, wrinkling his nose.

He read the sheet over twice, then folded it up and put it back in his pocket.

"Miss Cosentino is the same age as you, Chief. She was born here in February 1950. Only child. Her father was Angelo Cosentino, in the wood business, solid citizen, well respected and admired. Came from one of the oldest families in Vigàta.

When the Americans arrived in '43, they made him mayor. And he remained mayor till 1955. After that he wanted out of politics. The mother, Carmela Vasile-Cozzo —"

"What'd you say?" said Montalbano, who until that moment had been following him distractedly.

"Vasile-Cozzo," Fazio repeated.

She was probably related to Signora Clementina! If so, that would make everything easier.

"Wait a minute," he said to Fazio. "I have to make a phone call."

Signora Clementina sounded happy to hear Montalbano's voice.

"How long has it been since you last came to see me, you naughty man?"

"Please forgive me, signora, but work, you know. . . . Listen, are you by any chance a relative of Carmela Vasile-Cozzo, the mother of Mariastella Costentino?"

"Of course. First cousins, the daughters of two brothers. Why do you ask?"

"Signora Clementina, would you mind if I dropped by for a visit?"

"You know very well how much I enjoy seeing you. Unfortunately I can't invite you to lunch, because my son, his wife, and my grandson are here. But if you want to come by around four in the afternoon . . ."

"Thank you. See you later."

He hung up and looked pensively at Fazio.

"You know what I say? I say I don't need you anymore. Just tell me what the gossip is on Mariastella."

"What gossip? There's just the fact that she fell head over heels for Gargano. But they also say that there was never really anything between them."

"Okay, you can go."

Fazio went out, muttering to himself.

"The blessed guy made me waste the whole morning!"

At the Trattoria San Calogero the inspector ate so listlessly that even the owner noticed.

"Got worries?"

"A few."

He left and went for a walk along the jetty, out to the lighthouse.

He sat down on his customary rock and fired up a cigarette. He didn't want to think about anything. He just wanted to sit there and listen to the sea swashing between the rocks. But thoughts come even when you do all in your power to keep them away. And the thought that came into his mind concerned the Saracen olive tree

247

that had been cut down. Now he had only the rock for a refuge. All at once, though he was out in the open air, he felt strangely as though he were suffocating, as though the space allotted to his existence had suddenly shrunk. By a lot.

After they'd had their coffee and sat down in the living room, Signora Clementina began to speak.

"My cousin Carmela got married at a very young age, to Angelo Cosentino, who was a nice, educated, open-minded man. They had only one child, Mariastella. She was a pupil of mine, and had a peculiar temperament."

"In what sense?"

"Well, she was very closed, reserved. Almost sullen. She was also very formal. She later got an accounting degree at Montelusa. I think the fact that she lost her mother when she was only fifteen must have had a rather negative effect on her. From that moment on, she devoted herself to her father. She never went out of the house anymore."

"Were they well off financially?"

"They weren't rich, but I don't think they were poor, either. Five years after Carmela's death, Angelo also died.

Mariastella was twenty at the time, so she was no longer a little girl. But she acted like one."

"What did she do?"

"Well, when I found out that Angelo had died, I went to see Mariastella. I was with some other people, men as well as women. Mariastella came up to greet us, dressed in her usual fashion. She didn't wear black, not even when her mother died. Being her closest relative, I embraced her and tried to console her. But she stepped back from me and looked at me. 'Why, who died?' she asked. My blood ran cold, my friend. She couldn't accept that her father was dead. The problem continued —"

"For three days," said Montalbano.

"How did you know?" Clementina Vasile-Cozzo asked, astonished.

The inspector looked at her, even more astonished than she.

"Would you believe me if I told you that I don't know?"

"Well, it lasted indeed three days. We all tried to find ways to convince her, all of us: the priest, her doctor, me, the people from the funeral home. Nothing doing. Poor Angelo's body lay there on the bed, and Mariastella could not be persuaded to turn him over to the undertakers. Then — "

"— Right when you were about to resort to force, she gave in," said Montalbano.

"Well," said Mrs. Vasile-Cozzo, "if you know the story already, what point is there in my telling it to you?"

"Believe me, I don't know the story," said the inspector, feeling uneasy. "Yet it's as though somebody'd already told me the same story. Except that I can't remember how or where or why. Let's conduct an experiment. It seems to me that, if I ask you, say, 'Did you all begin to think that Mariastella was crazy?,' I already know your answer: 'We didn't think she was crazy. We thought there was an explanation for why she was behaving that way.' "

"You're right," said Signora Clementina, surprised. "That's exactly what we thought. Mariastella was rejecting reality with all her might. She was refusing to be an orphan, without another person to lean on in life."

But, good heavens, how did he know even the thoughts of the characters in the story? Around 1970, he and his father had already been away from Vigàta for years, and had no relatives or friends there, either. Therefore he couldn't have even heard the story from someone who'd experienced it directly. So what was the explanation?

"And what happened next?"

"For a few years Mariastella got by on the little her father had left her. Then a relative found her a position in Montelusa, and she worked there up to the age of forty-five. But she no longer socialized with anyone. Then, at a certain point, she quit her job. She explained — I forget to whom — that she'd quit because the drive to work and back frightened her. There was too much traffic, and this upset her."

"But it's barely six miles."

"What can I say? And to anyone who pointed out that to go into town, she also had to drive, she would reply that she felt safer on that road because it was familiar to her."

"And why did she decide to start working again? Did she need the money?"

"No. The whole time she'd been working in Montelusa she'd managed to put some money aside. I also think she had a small pension. Which, though small, was more than enough for her needs. No, she went back to work because Gargano sought her out."

Montalbano jumped straight out of his armchair, as though shot from a bow. Mrs. Vasile-Cozzo gave a start at the inspector's reaction and put a hand to her heart.

"They already knew each other?!"

"Please calm down, Inspector. You nearly gave me a heart attack."

"I'm sorry," said Montalbano, sitting back down. "I thought it was she who'd introduced herself to Gargano."

"No, here's how it went. The first time Emanuele Gargano came to Vigàta, he inquired as to the whereabouts of Angelo Cosentino, explaining that his uncle, the one who'd lived in Milan and brought him up, had told him that when Angelo was mayor he'd helped him out a great deal and saved him from bankruptcy. In fact, I myself remember that up until the 1950s there was a salesman named Filippo Gargano living in Vigàta. Anyway, Gargano was told that Angelo had passed away and that the only surviving family member was his daughter, Mariastella. Gargano was very keen to meet her and ended up offering her a job, which she accepted."

"Why?"

"You know, Inspector, Mariastella came to me herself and talked to me about this job. It was the last time I saw her. She never came to my house again. In any case, after her father's death we'd probably seen each other ten times, if that. The answer to your question, Inspector, is simple: She'd fallen naïvely and hopelessly in love with Gargano. It was clear to me from the way she talked about him. And I don't believe she'd ever had a boyfriend. Poor thing, you know what she's like . . ."

"But why?" Montalbano repeated.

Signora Clementina gave him a puzzled look.

"Didn't you hear what I said? Mariastella fell —"

"No, I'm wondering why a rogue like Gargano hired her. Out of gratitude? Let's not kid ourselves. Gargano's a shark. Who would slit the throats of his fellow sharks without a second thought. He had three employees in Vigàta. One of these, the one who was murdered, was a clever young man, very skilled at his job, though he pretended to be incompetent, or almost. But Gargano understood at once what he was made of. The other was a beautiful girl. In her case, too, one can understand why Gargano took her on. But Mariastella?"

"Out of self-interest," the woman said. "Pure self-interest. First of all, because in the eyes of the whole town, he would seem like a man who didn't forget anyone who had done him a favor, directly or indirectly. And this favor he repaid, in a sense, by hiring Mariastella. Don't you think that's a pretty good façade for a con artist? And, secondly, because it's always convenient for a man, con artist or no, to have a loving woman at his disposal."

He thought he remembered that the King Midas office closed at five-thirty. Chatting with Signora Clementina, he'd lost track of the time. He thanked her, said good-bye, promised to come back soon, got in his car, and left. Want to bet he would find the office already closed? Driving past King Midas, he saw Mariastella outside the already closed front door, rummaging through her purse, probably looking for the keys. He found a spot almost immediately, parked the car, and got out. Then everything began to happen as in a slow-motion sequence in a film. Mariastella was crossing the street, head down, without looking to either her left or her right. All at once she stopped, at the exact moment a car was coming. Montalbano heard the screech of the brakes, saw the car ever so slowly strike the woman straight on, and then saw her fall, also very slowly. The inspector started running and everything returned to its normal rhythm.

The driver got out and bent down over

Mariastella, who was lying on the ground, though moving, trying to get back up. Other people were rushing to the scene. The driver, a well-dressed man of about sixty, was scared to death and white as a sheet.

"She suddenly stopped!" he said. "I thought that —"

"Are you badly hurt?" Montalbano asked Mariastella, helping her get up. Then he turned to the others: "Go on home! It's nothing serious!"

Recognizing Montalbano, the people in the crowd that had formed began to disperse. The driver, however, didn't budge.

"What do you want?" Montalbano asked him as he was bending down to pick up Mariastella's purse.

"What do you mean, what do I want? I want to take the lady to the hospital!"

"I don't want to go to the hospital, I'm fine," Mariastella said firmly, looking to the inspector for support.

"No, I insist!" said the man. "What happened was not my fault! I want a medical report!"

"Why's that?" asked Montalbano.

"Because maybe later on, this same lady might quietly come out and say she suffered multiple fractures, and I'll be in hot water with my insurance!"

"If you're not out of my sight in one minute," said Montalbano, "I'm going to punch you in the face and you can bring me the medical report on that."

The man did not breathe a word, but simply got back in his car and drove off with a screech of the tires, something he'd probably never done before in his life.

"Thank you," said Mariastella, offering him her hand. "Good day."

"What are you going to do?"

"I'm going to get in my car and go home."

"Out of the question! You're in no condition to drive. Can't you see that you're trembling?"

"Yes, but that's normal. It'll pass in a few minutes."

"Listen, I helped you out by keeping you from going to the hospital. But now you must do as I say. I'll drive you home in my car."

"Yes, but how will I get to work tomorrow?"

"I promise that by this evening one of my men will have your car parked in front of your house. Now please give me the keys, so I don't forget. It's the yellow Fiat 500, isn't it?"

Mariastella Cosentino took the keys from her purse and handed them to the inspector. As they walked towards Montalbano's car, Mariastella was slightly dragging her left leg and holding her left shoulder very high, perhaps to lessen the pain.

"Would you like to take my arm?"

"No, thank you."

Polite and firm. If she'd taken the inspector's arm, what might people think, seeing her so free and easy with a man?

Montalbano held the car door open for her, and she got in, slowly and carefully.

She'd clearly taken a nasty hit.

Question: What should it have been Inspector Montalbano's duty to do?

Answer: To take the unhappy woman to the hospital.

Question: Then why didn't he do this?

Answer: Because, in fact, Mr. Salvo Montalbano, a worm in the guise of a police inspector, wanted to take advantage of Mariastella Cosentino's moment of trauma so that he could knock down her defenses and find out everything about her and her relations with Emanuele Gargano, con artist and murderer.

"Where does it hurt?" Montalbano asked as he put the key in the ignition.

"In my hip and my shoulder. But it's from the fall."

What she meant was that the sixty-year-old man's car had only given her a hard push, knocking her to the ground. It was her violent fall onto the pavement that had caused the damage. But it wasn't serious. She would wake up the following morning with her hip and shoulder a fine greenish-blue.

"Tell me where to go."

Mariastella instructed him to drive outside of Vigàta, having him turn onto a road with no houses but a few rare, solitary villas, some of them in a state of abandon. The inspector had never been down this road before, he was sure of it, because he felt astonished to find an area that remained as though frozen in a time before the so-called construction boom had turned everything into a wilderness of cement.

"Most of these villas you see were built in the late nineteenth century. They were the country homes of the rich of Vigàta. We turned down vast sums of money for ours. That's it over there."

Montalbano did not take his eyes off the road, but knew that *it was a big, squarish frame house that had once been white, decorated with cupolas and spikes and*

258

scrolled balconies in the heavily lightsome style of the seventies . . .

At last he looked up and saw the house. It was how he'd imagined it, only better. It corresponded perfectly, like an exact replica, with the image that had been suggested to him. But suggested by whom? Was it possible he'd seen that house before? No, he was certain he hadn't.

"When was it built?" he asked, afraid of the response.

"In 1870," said Mariastella.

16

"I haven't been upstairs for years and years," said Mariastella, opening up the massive front door. "I've settled in on the ground floor."

The inspector noticed the heavy iron grates over the windows. The upstairs windows were instead closed in by shutters of a now indeterminate color, with many missing slats. The plaster was flaking off the walls.

Mariastella turned round.

"If you'd like to come inside a minute . . ."

Her words were an invitation, but the woman's eyes said the exact opposite. They said: "For pity's sake, go away and leave me alone."

"Thanks," said Montalbano.

And he went inside. They crossed a large, unadorned foyer, *a dim hall from which a stairway mounted into still more shadow. It smelled of dust and disuse — a close, dank smell. Mariastella opened the door to the living room. It was furnished in heavy, leather-covered furniture*. The sort of nightmare he had suffered at Signora Clementina's place was becoming more and more oppressive. Inside his brain an unfamiliar voice said: "Look for the portrait." He obeyed. He looked all around, and, lo, *on a tarnished gilt easel before the fireplace stood a crayon portrait* of an elderly man with a mustache.

"Is that your father?" he asked, certain and yet at the same time frightened of the response.

"Yes," said Mariastella.

Montalbano now understood that he could no longer hold himself back, that he had to penetrate even further into that incomprehensible, dark area that lay between reality and what his own mind was suggesting to him, a reality that created itself as he was thinking it. He suddenly felt that he had a fever, and it was rising by the minute. What was happening to him? He didn't believe in magic spells, and yet at that moment he needed great faith in his own reason not to believe in them, and to keep both his feet on the ground. He realized he was sweating.

He'd had, in the past — however rarely — the experience of seeing a place for the first time and feeling as if he'd already been there, or of reliving situations he'd been in before. But this was something entirely different. The words that were coming back to him had never been said to him, never been uttered by a human voice. No, he was convinced he had read them somewhere. And these written words had so struck and perhaps troubled him that they had etched themselves in his memory. Forgotten, they were now returning with a vengeance. All at once he understood. Sinking into a fear of a sort he'd never felt or conceived before in his life, he understood. He realized he was living inside a fiction. He'd been transported inside a short story by Faulkner he'd read many years before. How was it possible? But this was no time for explanations. All he could do was to keep reading and living that story and arrive at its terrible conclusion, which he already knew. There was no other way. He stood up.

"I'd like you to show me your house."

She looked at him with surprise and some irritation at the violent manner in which the inspector had asked her to submit. But she didn't have the courage to say no.

"All right," she said, struggling to stand up.

The real pain of her fall was clearly

262

starting to make itself felt. Keeping one shoulder raised much higher than the other, and propping up her arm in one hand, she led Montalbano down a long corridor. She opened the first door on the left.

"This is the kitchen."

Very big, spacious, but seldom used. Hanging on one wall were some copper pots and pans that had turned almost white from the thick deposits of dust on them. She opened the door across the hall.

"This is the dining room."

Massive walnut furniture. It had probably been used once, maybe twice at the most, in the last thirty years. She reclosed the door.

They took a few more steps.

"Here on the left is the bathroom," said Mariastella.

But she didn't open the door. She took another three steps, then stopped in front of a closed door.

"This is my room. But it's messy."

She turned towards the door across from it.

"This is the guest room."

She opened the door, reached inside, turned on the light, then stood aside to let the inspector pass. *A thin, acrid pall as of the tomb seemed to lie everywhere upon this room . . .*

In a flash Montalbano saw what he was expecting to see: *Upon a chair hung the suit, carefully folded; beneath it the two mute shoes and discarded socks.*

And on a bed stained brown with dried blood, carefully wrapped in plastic and even more carefully sealed in adhesive tape, *lay the man himself,* Emanuele Gargano.

"There's nothing else to see," said Mariastella Cosentino, turning off the light in the guest room and closing the door. She turned, now listing to one side, and walked back up the corridor towards the living room. Montalbano, however, stayed put, in front of the closed door, unable to move, to take even one step. Mariastella had not seen the corpse. For her, it did not exist, it was not lying on that bloodstained bed. She had completely repressed it. As she had done, so many years before, with her father. The inspector heard a kind of storm howling inside his brain, windblown head in a windblown expanse, and was unable to form a sentence, to put two words together that might make some sense. Then a wail came to his lips, a kind of yowl, as of a wounded animal. He managed to take a step, wrenching himself painfully out of his paralysis, then ran to the living room. Mariastella was sitting in an armchair. She'd turned pale and was holding her shoulder with her right hand. Her lips were trembling.

"My God, I'm suddenly in such pain!"

"I'll call you a doctor," said the inspector, seizing upon that moment of normality.

"Please call Dr. La Spina," said Mariastella.

The inspector knew him. He was in his sixties and retired, but still treated his friends. He ran into the vestibule. There was a directory next to the telephone. He could hear Mariastella whimpering in the living room.

"Dr. La Spina? Montalbano here. Do you know Miss Mariastella Cosentino?"

"Of course, she's a patient of mine. Why, has something happened to her?"

"She was hit by a car and has a lot of pain in her shoulder."

"I'll be right over."

At this moment the solution he'd been so convulsively seeking occurred to him. He lowered his voice, hoping the doctor wasn't hard of hearing.

"Listen, Doctor. I'm going to ask a favor of you, for which I'll assume full responsibility. Please don't ask any questions now, but I need for Miss Mariastella to sleep very deeply for a few hours."

He hung up and took three or four deep breaths.

"He'll be right over," he said, going back into the living room and trying to assume as normal an attitude as possible. "Does it hurt very badly?"

"Yes."

When he later had to retell this story, the inspector could not remember what else they said to each other. Perhaps they had sat in silence. As soon as he heard a car pull up, Montalbano stood up and went to open the door.

"I mean it, Doctor, treat her, do whatever you need to do, but most important, put her into a deep sleep. It's for her own good."

The doctor looked him long in the eye, then decided not to ask any questions.

Montalbano waited outside, firing up a cigarette and pacing in front of the house. It was dark. The schoolmaster Tommasino came back to mind. What did the night smell of? He breathed deeply. It smelled of rotten fruit, of decomposition.

The doctor came out of the house about half an hour later.

"There's nothing broken. She has a nasty contusion on her shoulder, which I've wrapped up, and another on her hip. I persuaded her to get into bed and did as you asked. She's already asleep and should remain so for a few more hours."

"Thank you, Dr. La Spina. For your trouble, I'd like to —"

"Never mind about that. I've been her doctor since she was a little girl. But I don't feel right leaving her alone. I'd like to call a nurse."

"I'll be staying with her, don't worry about it."

They said good-bye. The inspector waited till the car was out of sight, then went back in the house and locked the door. Now came the hardest part, going back, of his own accord, into the nightmare of the fiction, becoming a character in the story again. He walked by Mariastella's room and saw her sleeping under a blanket *of faded rose color.* He saw *the rose-shaded lights . . . the dressing table . . . the delicate array of crystal . . .* Yet hers was not a placid sleep. Her long, iron-gray hair seemed to move continuously over the pillow. He made up his mind, opened the other door, turned on the overhead light, and went in. The wrapping sparkled from the reflections of the light off the plastic. He went up to it and bent down to have a look. Emanuele Gargano's undershirt was singed right over the heart; the bullet hole was clearly visible. He had not committed suicide. The pistol had been neatly placed on the other nightstand. Mariastella had shot him in his sleep. On the nightstand closer to the dead man lay a wallet and a Rolex. On the floor beside the bed was an open briefcase; inside were some computer diskettes and papers. Pellegrino's briefcase.

Now he had to bring the story to its conclusion. Was there, *in the second pillow . . . the indentation of a head?* And was there, on that same pillow, *a long strand of iron-gray hair?* He forced himself to look. There was no indentation, no strand of iron-gray hair on the pillow.

He breathed a sigh of relief. At least he'd been spared that. He turned off the light, closed the door, went back in Mariastella's room, pulled up a chair, and sat down beside her. Somebody had once told him that sedated sleep is dreamless. Then why was that poor body occasionally tossed and shaken by violent starts as if by a strong electrical charge? And that same somebody had also said that one could not truly cry in one's sleep. Then why were big tears seeping out from under the woman's eyelids? What did anyone, even scientists, know about what could happen in the mysterious, indecipherable, ineffable country of sleep? He took one of her hands in his. It was hot. He had overestimated Gargano. The man was only a con artist; the murder of Pellegrino had got to him. After pushing his car into the sea and seizing the briefcase, he had run to Mariastella, certain that she would never talk, never betray him. And Mariastella had welcomed him, consoled him, taken him in. Then, after she'd let him fall asleep, she shot him. Was it jealousy? A mad reaction to learning of her Emanuele's relationship with Giacomo? No, Mariastella would never have done that. Then he understood: She'd shot him out of love, to spare the only human being she'd ever really loved in her life the contempt, the dishonor, the imprisonment that awaited him. There could be no other explanation. The darker side of the inspector's mind (or perhaps the brighter) suggested a possible solution to him: Grab the whole package, put it in the trunk of his car, take it to the spot where Giacomo was murdered, and fling it into the sea. No one would ever suspect any involvement on Mariastella Cosentino's part. And he would have the pleasure of seeing the look on Guarnotta's face when he found Gargano's corpse carefully wrapped in plastic. Why had the Mafia wrapped him up? Guarnotta would ask himself in dismay.

But he was a cop.

He stood up. It was already eight o'clock. He went to the phone; maybe Guarnotta was still in his office.

"Hello, Guarnotta? Montalbano here."

He explained to him what he needed to do. Then he went back into Mariastella's room, wiped the sweat from her brow with a corner of the sheet, sat down, and again took one of her hands in his.

Then, after he didn't know how long, he heard the cars pull up. He opened the front door and went out to meet Guarnotta.

"Did you call an ambulance and a nurse?"

"They're on their way."

"Look around carefully. There's a brief-case in there that might help you recover the stolen money."

On the way back to Marinella, he had to pull over twice and stop. He was unable to drive. He was drained, and not just physically. The second time, he got out of the car. By now it was completely dark outside. He took a deep breath. And he noticed that the smell of the night had changed. It now had a light, fresh smell, a scent of young grass, citronella, and wild mint. He drove off again, exhausted but revived.

Upon entering his house, he froze. Livia was standing in the middle of the room, frowning, eyes flashing with anger. She was holding up with both hands the sweater he had forgotten to bury. Montalbano opened his mouth but no sound came out. Livia slowly lowered her arms, and her face changed expression.

"Oh my God, Salvo, what's wrong? What's happened?"

She threw the sweater to the ground and ran to embrace him.

"What's happened to you, darling? What's the matter?"

And she held him tight, desperate and frightened.

Montalbano was still unable to speak or return her embrace. He had only one thought in his mind, clear and strong:

It's a good thing she's here.

Author's Note

The idea of assigning Montalbano an investigation into the dealings of a financial "wizard" (a rather anomalous case, sort of a *divertissement*) came to me while reading an article by Francesco ("Ciccio," to friends) La Licata entitled "Multinational Mafia," which mentioned the case of one Giovanni Sucato (the "wizard"), who had "managed, through a kind of pyramid scheme in the millions, to build an empire. Then he was blown up in his car." My story is far more modest and, especially at the end, much different. Particularly different were my reasons for telling it. For here the Mafia have nothing to do with it, despite the convictions of Inspector Guarnotta, one of the characters. Nevertheless I must state that all names and situations are purely invented and have no basis in reality. Any similarity to real characters, etc. . . . The short story by William Faulkner that Montalbano finds himself living inside of is "A Rose for Emily."

Notes

13 ***ragioniere* Emanuele Gargano:** A *ragioniere* is someone who holds a degree in *ragioneria*, the study of business administration and accounting.

35 **two billion lire:** At the time this novel was written, right before the conversion to euros, it took about two thousand lire to equal one U.S. dollar. Thus two billion lire would have been worth about one million dollars.

35 a million lire . . . twenty billion lire: See note above. Twenty billion lire at the time would have equaled about ten million dollars.

44 ***lupara*:** A sawed-off shotgun, traditionally the weapon of choice among mafiosi and bandits in Sicily. It has since been replaced by more modern firearms.

45 **Lohengrin Pera, that son of a bitch from the Secret Service:** Coerced by Montalbano into making certain concessions against his will, the sinister Pera is an important minor character in Camilleri's *The Snack Thief* (Penguin, 2003).

51 **five hundred million lire:** About two hundred fifty thousand dollars at the time.

52 **tobacco shop:** Tobacco products are controlled by the government in Italy and sold in specially designated shops.

59 **who until six months ago had worked in Bolzano:** Bolzano is in a far northern, Alpine region of Italy where roughly half the population speaks German.

61 **Saying hello and good-bye must not be the rule around here:** In Italy it is customary for people, even clients, to greet each other upon entering and exiting places of public commerce such as shops and restaurants.

68 **as Orlando in fury had done with his sword:** A reference to the classic sixteenth-century Italian chivalric romance, *Orlando Furioso*, by Ludovico Ariosto (1434–1533).

83 **Turì . . . Turiddru:** Sicilian diminutives for the name Salvatore.

94 **D'Annunzio:** Gabriele D'Annunzio (1863–1938), an Italian poet and au-

thor much celebrated in his time, wrote a novel entitled *Forse che sì, forse che no* (*Maybe Yes, Maybe No*), published in 1910.

97 **salary of two million two hundred thousand lire:** About one thousand one hundred dollars.

99 **The tombs shall open, the dead shall rise:** A line from the Italian national anthem, often ironically quoted to express astonishment at the occurrence of an unusual event.

101 *nunnatu:* Sicilian for *neonato* (i.e., "newborn"). Calogero is referring to tiny baby fish that one is not allowed to catch except on occasions such as the one alluded to here. Also called *cicirella* (or *cicireddra*).

114 *patati cunsati:* Seasoned potatoes.

120 **"May you bear only sons":** The full expression, uttered often as a toast at weddings, is *auguri e figli maschi* (literally, "best wishes and male children").

135 **a debate between those in favor and those against building a bridge over the Strait of Messina:** Whether or not to build a bridge over the turbulent Strait of Messina, site of the passage between Scylla and

Charybdis in ancient Greek myth, has long been a subject of public debate in Italy. Most recently Prime Minister Silvio Berlusconi, even while slashing social benefits and privatizing many state-run industries, has revived the project to span the Strait, as part of a broad public-works program intended above all to serve his own greater glory. Camilleri's reference to the question should be seen in this context.

146 Punta Raisi: The airport of Palermo.

164 "Excursion to Tindari": *Excursion to Tindari* (Penguin, 2004) is the previous book in the Inspector Montalbano series.

175 "Thirty million lire": About fifteen thousand dollars.

178 *Nottata persa e figlia femmina*: Literally: "a night lost, and it's a girl." A Sicilian saying first quoted by Camilleri in *Excursion to Tindari*, it means more or less "what a lot of wasted effort." As the narrator explains in that book, it is "the proverbial saying . . . of the husband who has spent a whole night beside his wife in labor, only to see her give birth to a baby girl instead of that much-desired son."

189 **"La donna è mobile":** Aria from Giuseppe Verdi's opera *Rigoletto*.

193 **the violin of Maestro Cataldo Barbera:** A reference to the reclusive violinist of Camilleri's *Voice of the Violin* (Penguin, 2003), whose virtuosic skills ultimately inspire Inspector Montalbano to solve the case of that book.

213 ***pasta 'ncasciata:*** One of the many forms of southern Italian *pasta al forno,* that is, a casserole of oven-baked pasta and other ingredients. *Pasta 'ncasciata* generally contains small macaroni, *tuma* or *caciocavallo* cheese, ground beef, mortadella or salami, hard-boiled eggs, tomatoes, eggplant, grated Pecorino cheese, basil, olive oil, and a splash of white wine.

216 **"Seven hundred million lire in all":** About three hundred and fifty thousand dollars.

223 **"that guy who was found hanged under the Blackfriars' Bridge. . . . that other guy, the one who faked being kidnapped by the Mafia, shot himself in the leg, and then drank a cup of poisoned coffee in prison . . .":** The man found hanged

under the Blackfriars' Bridge was Roberto Calvi, president of the Banco Ambrosiano, a bank with ties to the Vatican, not to mention a host of holdings in offshore companies and Swiss bank accounts, and closely connected to a shadowy network of secret Masonic lodges, mafiosi, politicians, and arms traders. The second man Montalbano alludes to was Michele Sindona, a financier at the center of a similar, and indeed related, web of interests. It was, in fact, while investigating Sindona that the Italian courts eventually discovered the existence of the famous P2 Masonic lodge — whose membership included industrial barons, intelligence men, neo-Fascists, mafiosi, and numerous politicians — triggering a scandal that would ultimately spell the ruin, in the early 1990s, of the Christian Democratic Party, which had dominated the Italian government since the end of the Second World War.

225 **"So he plays the fool, as the saying goes, to avoid going to war"**: *Fa u fissa pi nun iri a la guerra*. A Sicilian-Calabrian expression that essentially means to feign ig-

norance or to "play dumb."

244 *"O Gesù biniditto!"*: O blessed Jesus! (Sicilian dialect).

246 **"Signora Clementina"**: Clementina Vasile-Cozzo is a character in both *The Snack Thief* and *Voice of the Violin* and a friend of Inspector Montalbano.

Notes by Stephen Sartarelli

About the Author

ANDREA CAMILLERI is the author of many books, including his Montalbano series, which has been adapted for Italian television and translated into nine languages. He lives in Rome.

STEPHEN SARTARELLI is an award-winning translator. He is also the author of three books of poetry, most recently *The Open Vault*.